IT MIGHT HAVE BEEN

Lloyd J. Schwartz

authorHOUSE®

AuthorHouse™
1663 Liberty Drive
Bloomington, IN 47403
www.authorhouse.com
Phone: 833-262-8899

Published by AuthorHouse 11/15/2024

ISBN: 979-8-8230-3727-3 (sc)
ISBN: 979-8-8230-3728-0 (hc)
ISBN: 979-8-8230-3729-7 (e)

Library of Congress Control Number: 2024923508

Print information available on the last page.

Any people depicted in stock imagery provided by Getty Images are models, and such images are being used for illustrative purposes only. Certain stock imagery © Getty Images.

Cover Art: Joanie Coyote

This book is printed on acid-free paper.

For my grandparents, parents, wife, sons, daughters-in-law, and grandsons. My grandparents inspired this story. My parents, wife, children, and grandchildren inspire me.

CHAPTER ONE

Genial, middle-aged attorney Nathan Glass slides into the First National Bank through the side entrance as he often does, but somehow this day is different. As always, he nods to Archie, the bank security officer, but this time he doesn't stop to chat—much too much on his mind. The perceptive Archie notices the difference in Nathan, but what the hell; not everyone can be in a good mood all the time. Banks do that to people. Archie tosses his glance to another customer.

Nathan takes out his key ring even before he approaches the bank manager. It takes Nathan a moment before he actually locates the key to the safety deposit box. His house key, his office key, the key to his Chevy, his key to his home safe—he uses every key more often than the key to the safety deposit box at the bank.

Amadou, the bank manager from Mali, looks up and sees Nathan. Nathan and his whole family had banked at this branch even before Amadou immigrated, even before he was a teller. Amadou grins familiarly at Nathan and pushes aside some papers on his desk.

He gets up to intercept Nathan in the middle of the bank before he can approach the centerline. "Mr. Glass, I don't usually see you in the bank on a Monday."

Nathan displays his safety deposit box key. "It's not for a deposit or withdrawal."

Amadou looks at the key on the key ring in Nathan's hand. "I see. I can help you with that."

Amadou takes out his own set of keys and escorts Nathan to the secure area where the safety deposit boxes are. Amadou opens the gate and leads

Nathan. Following procedure, Amadou locks the gate and door after them. Amadou takes Nathan's key ring from his hand and seeks out the number leading to Nathan's box. There are different sizes of safety deposit boxes, and Nathan's is the largest kind.

"Here it is: 6324."

Amadou uses the two corresponding keys to unlock the space. As he pulls out the box, he sees the sudden sorrow on Nathan's face. Everyone at the bank had liked Nathan's mother. Joining in Nathan's grief, he says, "She was a nice woman."

"Better than that: A great woman. She endured a lot."

Nathan's mother was not one to share what her life had been like. And following suit, this was the first time Nathan even so much as mentioned his mother's travails. Amadou only knew her from the times he saw her in the bank. "I liked your mother. Rita Glass always thanked everyone for everything."

Amadou hands the box to Nathan, and they place it on the table in the center of the vestibule.

"How old was she? I never could tell."

"She never told me. One thing about my mother: She was good at keeping secrets."

The two men stare at each other. They both now assume a more professional demeanor.

Amadou, now the banker manager again, says, "Let me know when you're done."

Nathan watches Amadou leave the area and close the door and gate behind him.

Nathan pauses as he peers at the box on the table in front of him. It's as if he's alone with his mother, yet somehow this feels like a violation. He puts those feelings aside and turns to the matter at hand. He inhales without exhaling—as if he were holding his breath in a swimming pool—and then opens the box. He takes out a few pieces of jewelry, insurance forms, her marriage licenses, and then a large, aged envelope. If he were to open it, he'd see that it contains an extensive diary and letters, lots of letters. Written on the envelope in his mother's scrawled handwriting: "For Nathan. To be opened after Nathan's death."

Naturally, he is curious about the envelope. He takes it and replaces the other items in the box, closes the lid, and then looks around for Amadou. For some reason Nathan feels he needs to leave the bank quickly, as well as leaving the other safety deposit boxes around him.

With the envelope perched on the passenger seat next to him, Nathan drives out of the parking lot and enters traffic for the short ride home. He turns on the radio and listens to the classical station that he and his mother used to listen to together. Then, just as quickly, he turns it off. He looks over at the envelope, as if to apologize for removing it from its safekeeping.

He turns into the driveway of his comfortable home. If he looks carefully at the living room window, he can see his wife, Linda, looking out from behind the curtain. She knows what his mission was and is equally curious about the result of his trip to the bank.

Before Nathan can even put the key in the door, Linda opens it for him. She is focused on the envelope. "That's all that was in the box?"

"No. There were some other things, but this … this was something I never saw before."

"Why didn't you open it there?"

"I thought we should wait so we could see what's in it together."

Linda thinks about it before concluding, "Then let's wait till after we eat."

"Why not? We've waited this long. I didn't even remember she had a safety deposit box until I found the key."

Linda takes the envelope from him and places it on the credenza in the dining room as she continues through the kitchen. From there, she opens the back door and steps out onto the porch. "Matthew! Deborah! Come in and wash up for dinner!"

Matthew is eleven, and Deborah is five. Though they are often at odds, today they are playing together in the backyard where Matthew is showing Deborah how to throw a Frisbee.

"Hold it flat and then kind of flick it with your wrist."

Deborah yells back at her mother, "Do we have to?"

"Yes. Both. Wash up and have dinner."

One more throw from Deborah.

"Much better, Deborah. If we eat fast, we can play some more before the sun goes down."

Another throw from Matthew to Deborah, who misses catching it before they trot to the house.

After dinner and after the kids had gone to bed, Linda and Nathan peer over at the envelope, which had been looming on the credenza, beckoning to them clear through dessert. Now the moment has come. Almost in a whisper, Linda says, "I guess we can open it."

Nathan says, "I think we should."

As Nathan pulls at the strings around the old envelope, Linda grabs his shoulder. "Wait."

Nathan pauses. "What's the matter?"

"Before we look at what's inside, did you read what it says on the outside? That we shouldn't open it until after my mother has passed away."

"No, that's not what it says."

Now they both look at the written message—a message in Nathan's mother's handwriting that they know so well. It says, "For Nathan. To be opened after Nathan's death."

Linda confirms it. "Not after your mother's death. After Nathan's death. And '*for Nathan*.' That's what it says."

Much as they'd like to see the contents of the envelope, they both realize they can't open it. They know they have to obey his mother's last request. They agree that Nathan should return the envelope to the safety deposit box in the bank in the morning. That way they won't be tempted to open it.

CHAPTER TWO

(As told by Matthew Alan Glass)

I didn't know my grandmother very well. I mean, I knew her as a grandmother, but not as a person. She died when I was only seven. She was *Grita*. When I first started to talk, Grita was as close as I could come to annunciating Grandma Rita. It's funny since after I started calling her Grita, everyone in the family did too. Now that I'm twenty and there is all this talk about the envelope and what she had put inside it, I wish I would have asked her a lot of questions. But I was only seven, so what kind of questions would a seven-year-old ask of a woman who was in her nineties?

I'm rambling a little. The last three months have been really hard on my mom, my sister, and me. When we got the call about the car accident, my sister, Deborah, and I aged quickly. You never expect that one day would change everything about everything.

We were packing to go to Mexico for a vacation. Dad really values our family vacations. Since he's a partner at the law firm, he doesn't take a lot of vacations, so everyone was special for him and the family.

I am fair-skinned, and we heard the Mexican sun can really burn. Dad ran out to buy some sunscreen. It's not like they don't have sunscreen in Acapulco, but Dad just jumped up and said he'd go get some. I think he was getting jumpy, since the rest of us were still figuring out what to bring, and it gave him something to do in the meantime. That's what Dad would always say: "In the meantime." God, I'm going to miss him saying "in the meantime."

So for the last three months we've been trying to figure it all out. Dad had always taken care of just about everything. First, there was his funeral. He would have known exactly what to do about that.

I had heard that Grita, at one time, was an event planner. She would have known what to do. Mom did her best, and her twin sister, Darlene, came in to help out with the details before the rest of her family joined us here.

So many people came to the service. Dad was loved. I mean really loved—and not just by my mom and sister but people at his law firm. They came from all around: Cousins I had never met before all said great things about Nathan Glass. Stories and jokes about him as a lawyer and a person. I laughed. I cried, and I laughed. I guess it was okay to laugh. It stopped me from crying so much. People were as nice as they could be.

Then, at our house, a lot of people came up to talk to me, but nobody knew exactly what to say. Especially my friends. Nobody ever had a dad die before. I tried to be strong, and sometimes I was. Most of the time I wasn't.

I still cry. Now, a little less. Mom tries to be strong for Deborah and me. She says we have to get on with our lives. She says that, and then she cries. Now a little less, too. Not much less, but less.

There were forms and things and wills and things I never understood. I still don't understand, but I've been told that we'll be fine, that we're taken care of.

Our lawyer, Mr. Howard—one of Dad's partners at the law firm and a good friend of Dad's—told me, "You're fine all the way through law school if you want to be a lawyer like your dad."

Then he said, "In the meantime …"

How could he say, "In the meantime"?

I really lost it. I was going to hit him or something, but Mom pulled me away and calmed me down, and Deborah held me. I yelled at her, "How could he say, 'In the meantime'!"

Deborah and I have gotten so close going through this. We have always been close, but now closer. We'll make it okay, I guess. Dad raised us to be strong, and I am. Sometimes.

But now we've all been thinking more and more about Grita's envelope. I didn't know anything about it until Mom mentioned it Tuesday. She knew the time had come for her to go to the bank to get the envelope and see what that diary and those letters said and why they couldn't be read until after Dad died. We'll soon find out.

CHAPTER THREE

The Ukraine was cold when it wasn't even cold. There was not much to say about the quality of life there at the beginning of the last century. People were born there, and after that, they just did what they had to do to get by until they died. Work, sleep, and then work again until their years disappeared as quickly as summers.

Most of the people were farmers who brought their crops to a central market in Bukachivtski, like they did everywhere across Russia in any of the equally impoverished shtetls that sprinkled the countryside.

Bukachivtski wasn't special. The people weren't special, but then again, nobody was special to Tsar Nicholas II, who only viewed the Russian people as the source of his wealth when he viewed them at all. That was why, after a day of grueling work in the fields, everyone's favorite recreation in Bukachivtski was to gather in one of their small homes and complain about their lives and the Tsar. Then they inhaled the possibility of freedom and all talk of America.

Some of the relatives of the citizens of Bukachivtski had gone to America and wrote back about the opportunities there. *Opportunities* was one word for which there was no accurate Russian translation, because opportunities were something that no one had in the Ukraine unless and until they would leave their homeland.

No matter how hard your life is, leaving one's homeland isn't an easy thing to do since one's homeland is all anyone knows. And going to America for most of the people of Bukachivtski was a dream bigger than they were, but still, it was something they all dreamed. In the fields, they often pulled up their beets, paused, smiled, and said, "America." The harder life became for them, the easier it was to say, "America." Sometimes they just smiled at each other, and that meant "America" too. shetl

Two young people from Bukachivtski are Daniel Stabinski and Rita Rabinovich. Life is a bit easier for them because they have each other. Daniel is smart, with the kind of blazing blue eyes that let anyone who meets him know just how bright he is. If he wasn't working in the field every day, he could have a rosy future. He knows it. Now he just farms and brings in the crops while he imagines a life faraway … a life with Rita … maybe in America.

Rita shares his dreams. The overriding dream that the two have is to share one life. Rita is a beautiful young woman. At seventeen years, most of the people of Ukraine have already used up half their lives, since old people are a rarity in this land, where life is made more difficult because of the infirmities that come with old age.

The only place the old people of Bukachivtski are at peace is the cemetery of the shtetl. That's where Daniel's mother and father are buried. They died trying to keep warm when their house caught fire four years ago, and they perished before anyone could save them. Daniel was in the fields at the time and didn't know they died and found the ashes of his home and of his parents when he returned to a home that would never be again.

Daniel and Rita met in school at six years old. In Bukachivtski, school only lasts until children reach twelve. Everything they know after that is the education that comes from backbreaking work in the fields.

Since Daniel and Rita turned twelve, they had been trading books back and forth. That's how they grew so close. They also learned about life and love and grew mature beyond their years. Books and each other. That's what Daniel and Rita have.

Rita was there for Daniel when the fire destroyed his life, and he would have to face the future without his parents. That was four years ago. And that, too, brought them closer.

It is now February 16, 1903, and Daniel is returning from the fields. The beets are hearty, but this cold might be too hard for them to fight off. There was not much that Daniel could do, but he had gone to the field, nonetheless. He lights a fire of beechwood that he hacked from trees in a nearby grove in hopes that the smoke would raise the temperature enough to make a difference to the crop. If not, maybe just letting the beets know he was there—that he cared—would make some kind of difference.

Daniel can't wait to wash up in the river before he sees Rita later. The river is nearly frozen…but seeing her will be worth any temporary discomfort.

He is on the path down toward the river when he hears the pounding of the hooves of a horse on the dirt road above him. Then when it draws closer, Daniel hears the grunts from the horse's lungs as he sees the smoke-like breath of an animal that has been ridden too hard. Daniel turns in time to see the horse pass him. He knows the rider is Ivan, the cursed tax collector.

Ivan has never bothered to come to where Daniel lives because even the government has a way of knowing that Daniel has nothing. Ivan's horse rushes toward Bukachivtsi, where its rider will make the lives of the people of the shtetl even more miserable than it already is.

Daniel trails Ivan into town. Ivan passes house after house. Daniel's only concern is Rita. Daniel's fear is that Ivan will be stopping at Rita's house. Sadly, that is just where the taxman is going. When Daniel reaches the Rabinovich house, he sees Ivan's sweating white horse pawing at the ground where it is tied to the post outside.

Daniel doesn't dare look in the window since he might be seen, and that would give away too much. Not only is Daniel afraid of being spotted by Ivan, he doesn't want Rita's father and mother to know that he continues to exist in Rita's life.

Years ago, when Daniel and Rita were twelve, they used to be friends openly. Then Rita's parents, Abraham and Esther, made it clear to their daughter that they didn't approve of him. It's not that they didn't like Daniel as a person. They didn't know him well enough to like or dislike him. It was just that Daniel's parents didn't have a shekel, and it was important to Rita's father that she marry someone with a future. That's what Rita told him her father said. At twelve, Daniel didn't know what a future was, but he could tell when somebody didn't want him around.

He was already used to being disregarded since the day he became an orphan. Indeed, Abraham Rabinovich knows Daniel's prospects are even less promising since he has no father or mother to fall back on.

Ever since Daniel was fourteen, he moved from one relative's house to another, and he is always that extra mouth to feed. Through it all, Daniel and Rita have remained friends—but they never let anyone else know.

They keep their relationship to themselves. They always know in their hearts that they will be married one day, so until that time, they didn't see any reason to upset Rita's parents.

The only time they left the little shtetl together was when they went to the large city of Botosani. Rita had told her father she was visiting a cousin; instead, she and Daniel enjoyed being in each other's company in a different place. Daniel had scratched together enough money to pay a photographer to take their picture, and that photograph would soon become Daniel's prized possession.

That was months ago. Now Daniel would have burst into the Rabinovich home if he saw the way that Ivan was treating Rita and her parents. A taxman in the Ukraine was the only authority from St. Petersburg the people of the shtetl ever saw, and Ivan uses his position to lord it over anyone who owes money to the Tsar. Rita and her parents cower against the wall as Ivan struts around the room as if he owned their house and their lives—which in some way he did.

Though Abraham is only sixty-one, he has aged well beyond his years, and the downtrodden Esther huddles next to her husband. Nearby is the youthful Rita, who fairly glows in comparison. Her vibrancy and beauty do not go unnoticed by Ivan, who has taken time from his collection to eye the attractive young woman.

Ivan's interest in Rita is more lascivious than anyone in the family appreciates. Abraham does what he can to bring Ivan back to the reason he has come to their house.

Speaking Russian: *"We gave what we could."*

Ivan scoffs out a response. *"What you 'could' is still not enough. The Tsar and I demand full payment."* This brings Ivan around to look at Rita once again, and he says menacingly and pointedly, *"And I demand payment, too."*

Esther and Abraham see where Ivan's gaze is focused, and they clutch Rita more closely than they already were. Abraham turns to his wife and hopes that a bribe will satisfy Ivan. With Ivan distracted by Rita, Abraham whispers to Esther, *"Bring me the cedar box."*

Abraham says to Ivan, *"Can we talk about this?"*

Esther slips into the bedroom, where she removes a floorboard and pulls out a small cedar box. Holes under the floor in the houses in Bukachivtsi are all the banks that anyone has.

Esther returns to the room just as Ivan moves toward Rita. She hands the box to her husband, who takes out some rubles and hands them to Ivan as if he had somehow just discovered them. Ivan looks at the coins in his hand and shakes his head. It's still not enough.

Abraham quickly empties the rest of their holdings.

Seeing that there is nothing left in the box, Ivan says, *"This will do— for now."*

Ivan gives a parting glance at Rita and then leaves without another word.

Abraham opens his arms, and both Esther and Rita enfold in his embrace. Though they are safe for at least one more visit by Ivan, at one level, Abraham feels he is letting down his wife and daughter by not protecting them more.

*

Outside the Rabinovich house, Ivan gets on his horse. If he had looked around, he would have seen that he had almost knocked over Daniel as he got in the saddle. Ivan kicks his horse and moves to the next hovel. Daniel can only hope that it hasn't been too bad for the Rabinovitch family. And that Ivan had left them with more than their dignity.

The next day, while working in the field, Daniel sees Abraham pass by on the road. Abraham has detached his horse from the plow, so it must be important, or Abraham would never give up a day of work. Daniel tries to shrug off the observation, but somehow, he knows that Abraham is on a mission.

If Daniel were only to know how critical Abraham's unusual trip is to Daniel's own future, he would have done everything and anything to stop him.

In the afternoon of the next day, Daniel and Rita meet behind the school where they always meet. And like always—unseen—they climb the hill, where sunflowers are blooming, which rises from the shtetl. She seems to be hurried … no, anxious. No, both. Daniel senses it, but neither talks about it.

When they reach the crest, they look down on the town and see a different Bukachivtski. Whereas before the main street had always been clear of any wagons, now near each house, goods are loaded in carts.

Furniture, tools, and clothes are stacked every which way. Such as it is at the Rabinovich house as well. Perhaps Daniel is too caught up in Rita's eyes to comment on the change in Bukachivtski.

Perhaps he has seen it and prefers to fool himself into thinking that it means nothing. At any rate, Ivan's visit has prompted immediate action from the people of Bukachivtski.

There is a copse of trees that Daniel and Rita have proclaimed to be their place. It is here among the beds of sunflowers where they have always been free from the cares that Bukachivtski has imposed upon them.

Rita pulls Daniel along and then down next to her on the soft, foliage-covered ground. Daniel knows her well enough to sense that something definitely has changed—and not in a good way. *"Rita, what's the hurry?"*

She answers cryptically, *"We don't have any time."*

Now Daniel takes a long look at all the loaded wagons on the street. Daniel says, *"Why? All of us are leaving. We will be going together to America. I will make it easy for us. You know I study English. And maybe be a doctor."* He shows off by speaking in English for the first time: "Hello, friends."

Rita smiles at his attempt at language skills, but only for a moment before she says, *"Oh, Daniel, kiss me."*

He does. It is completely filled with love. She holds the kiss so extraordinarily long that he finally must come up for air. He starts to laugh and then stops when he sees that she has tears in her eyes.

"Rita, why are you like this? What's wrong?"

Rita knows that what she is about to say will crush Daniel. The knowledge of what she will tell him has already crushed her. Yet, the time has run out. She can do nothing but tell him. *"I'm getting married tomorrow."*

At first, Daniel can't comprehend what she is saying. He just looks into her eyes. She looks away. *"Don't joke with me."*

She can't bear to be looking at him as she lets it all out in a single breath—as if the message will be less painful that way. *"Oh, Daniel, my papa has arranged my wedding to Mikal Gleisserman. Mama told me only last night. And the wedding is to be tomorrow, so Mikal and I will travel to America as husband and wife."*

Daniel is shocked and then angry as he gradually sinks to the ground in front of her. He can barely get out what he needs to say. *"This cannot be. Our plans ... we have plans. We made plans."*

Every single word that Rita utters is like an individual blade entering his soul. *"My papa arranged it. Mikal makes a good living. Papa wants that life for me."*

At this time in Russia, arranged marriages were not uncommon. Perhaps Abraham had always planned to marry off his Rita this way. It had never been discussed in their home. It had never been important before, but with the mounting pressure from the Tsar, everyone in the village was making decisions that they hadn't planned to make.

Daniel remembers Abraham riding past him the previous day and realizes that that was where Rita's father was going. He was arranging her marriage to this Mikal and thus ending Daniel and Rita's dreams.

Daniel is unrealistic when he pressures her further. *"But what do you want?"*

"It doesn't matter what I want—what we want. It is the way. We always knew this could happen."

Daniel is not strong enough to go on with any kind of argument. It's futile. As his life disappears in front of him, he can only manage a *"But our plans!"*

Rita is now suddenly the mature one. She says, *"That was yesterday … when we were young."*

"Who is this Mikal Gleisserman? Other than a man who makes a good living and is ending our dream."

"I don't know. I never saw him in all my life. He is a shopkeeper, is twenty-six, and from Shtetl Berdichev."

Daniel moves away from her. She can't stand looking at his back, knowing that he is turning from her.

She turns to him and pulls him close. *"I love you, Daniel."*

His tears make it worse for both of them. She moves her hand to his face. She isn't sure if she wants to wipe his tears away or collect them—to keep them. Instead, he moves her hands down his body. They had never made love before, but she had felt him. And suddenly, they both know what is going to happen. They want to. They need to. Nothing could be righter than to make this physical conclusion to their relationship.

They kiss and continue to kiss as they undress each other silently and never look at each other's bodies until they are completely naked. Then they stop and gaze at each other unashamedly.

Before she opens her arms to him welcomingly, he looks deeply into her eyes. His question is obvious. She smiles. Her answer is obvious.

Though this is her first time, the pain of their parting is far worse than the pain of her losing her innocence. In a way, her innocence was lost when her father told her that she would be marrying someone else, someone other than the person she has always loved.

Daniel tells her, *"I love you, Rita."*

"I love you, Daniel. No one could love you as much as I do. I always have, and I always will."

There is physical pain for Rita since it is her first time, but somehow even that is right since it is also the emotional pain that will last for their lifetimes. These are precious moments since this one time is all they would ever have to sanctify what they have meant to each other and will continue to mean to each other.

After he loses himself within her, they hold each other as tightly as they can. Even so, they know that they can never seal off the outside world that will shortly destroy what they have had.

They remain embraced for a full hour until the sun begins to create the long shadows on the shtetl. They both know they must return there, but they can't bear to pull away from each other since they also know that when they do, nothing will ever be the same.

Finally, Rita makes the first move. *"I have to go."*

"I know."

As if they were an old married couple, they hand each other their clothing caringly, lovingly. They say no more words to each other. Nothing else needs to be said. Daniel looks away as Rita puts on her clothes and he puts on his. It is a moment that would never be theirs after this time.

He kisses her sweetly and then turns away. She backs away from him and continues looking at him as she moves silently down the hill.

Daniel waits for a while. Then he kneels and picks up some dirt in his hand. He looks at the soil. This is earth from their place. It's all he has left of Rita as it crumbles through his fingers onto the ground.

*

The next morning, Daniel wakes up in the one-room shack that has served as his home for the last few months. The small window lets in the light of Rita's wedding day. Daniel doesn't move from his straw bed. He just stares at the ceiling. He determines to remain that way until most of the day is gone. He'll just lie there thinking about what might have been.

Outside the temple in Bukachivtski, all loading of wagons has been suspended as a wedding is taking place. Most of the town knows the Rabinovich family. Not only is this the occasion of a wedding, but this probably will be the last such ceremony as the people of the entire town will be leaving shortly to make their way to Hamburg and from there to America.

Inside, the rabbi looks at Mikal Gleisserman in front of him. The twenty-six-year-old Mikal seems a pleasant enough man. The rabbi has known Rita her entire lifetime. He had presided over all the significant events for the Rabinovich family: births, bar mitzvahs, deaths. He had comforted them when Nahem, the two-year-old light of their life, had died during the epidemic seven years ago.

And now both men wait for Rita to come down the aisle. One man has known her for many years. The other man has never met her and will be marrying her.

Neither the rabbi nor anyone in the town had seen the man until this day.

He is from Berdichev, another shtetl. Berdichev is slightly bigger than Bukachivtski and is only sixty kilometers away, but it is a full day's journey since the roads are little more than ox paths. Mikal Gleisserman is only known by Rita's father. As a shopkeeper, Mikal has more money than most of the men in Berdichev, and that would be enough for Rita's father. Abraham had asked several people about Mikal's character. No one had anything bad to say about him. "No one had anything bad to say" is enough of a recommendation since Abraham wanted everything settled— and settled quickly.

With a nod from the rabbi to the viola player at the rear of the synagogue, the ceremony begins. Being deep-throated, a viola is not the most appropriate solo instrument for a wedding, but the rest of the musician's string compatriots had already left for the coast city to find room on a departing ship.

There are no groomsmen; there are no bridesmaids. Rita walks gracefully with her mother. Rita neither smiles nor frowns. She is doing her duty as a daughter in a society that honors traditions. In this case, the tradition of arranged marriage has torn a young woman from the man she loves and marries her off to a man whom she has never met.

Rita reaches the front of the synagogue, and Abraham stands from his place and moves next to his daughter.

The ceremony is performed by the rabbi in an odd mix of Yiddish, Russian, and biblical Hebrew, which the rabbi blends expertly. He even jokes that soon all of them will have to learn yet another language when they move to America.

Rita sees no humor in the ceremony. She thinks that the less she listens, the less she will have to remember. She steals a look or two at her groom. He is shorter than Daniel. He is older than Daniel. His eyes don't flash like Daniel's.

Everything about this Mikal Gleisserman she compares unfavorably to Daniel, yet it is Mikal she is marrying.

At the end of the ceremony, the rabbi places down the glass for the groom to break. He points out that this tradition signifies that even at happy events, we must all remember that there is pain in the world. The irony is not lost on Rita, who cannot help but think of the pain that Daniel must be feeling at this moment.

Rita is not wrong, since at that exact moment, Daniel is in their place on the hill. He has been to enough weddings to have figured out that this is about the time when the rabbi will be pronouncing the love of his life and a man she never met *husband and wife.* That pronouncement and the ensuing breaking of the glass will make it official, and Rita will be married to someone else. When Mikal stamps down and breaks the ceremonial glass, he breaks Daniel's heart as well.

The people of the congregation respond with "mazel tov." Everyone— except for Rita—is pleased with the union. It will be good for all of them.

Though all will be happy, and another couple will be married; on the hill, Daniel is crushed and cannot believe he will ever recover.

The viola player begins a recessional, and the groom takes the arm of his new bride. Other than a peck of a kiss in the ceremony, this is the first time he has ever touched her. Barely looking at each other, they walk down the aisle and out the door of the synagogue.

Outside, a wagon with two horses stands ready to take them back to a hotel somewhere between his shtetl and her shtetl where they will spend their wedding night. Then, the next day, they will return as their honeymoon will be on the road to Hamburg and then on the ocean as Rita's family and Mikal's family make the voyage to America.

As Rita is helped into the wagon by Mikal and her family surrounds them, she glances toward the hill where she and Daniel had spent so much time together. He never told her that was where he would be. He never had to. It's too far for her to make him out distinctly, but it is confirmed for her when she sees a rustling in the leaves and a distant figure … as Daniel moves away.

Mikal doesn't know why, but he can tell that his new wife is troubled. As they get in the waiting coach, he turns to her gently. *"I hope you will learn to love me."*

He kisses her tenderly and then paternally on the top of her head. They say very little in the coach on the way from the synagogue. Finally, Rita speaks first. *"Where are we going?"*

"This is our wedding night. We must be alone to consummate our marriage."

As Rita will learn, Mikal always speaks his mind directly. Rita doesn't know how to respond to his bluntness and decides to say nothing more.

Mikal has made all the arrangements at an inn that is on the way to the coast. It is the practical thing to do, because above all else, Mikal is both direct and practical. Practicality is one of the reasons Mikal married Rita. He believes it would be most practical for them to enter America as a married couple. It cost him more in the dowry than he paid Abraham, but it made sense. Making sense and being practical are what helped make Mikal the richest man in Berdichev. Of course, being the richest man in impoverished shtetls is not a major accomplishment.

When Mikal and Rita enter the inn, Rita cannot help but be impressed. Though the establishment is not glamorous in any way, it is the nicest place Rita has ever been. There are plush divans in the lobby with a preponderance of tattered doilies on the divans as well as on the chairs, tables, and clerk's desk. Rita surmises that making doilies must be the hobby of the owner's wife.

Mikal already has the key, and the newlyweds make their way through the large sitting room on their way to the bridal suite. He says proudly, *"The bridal suite. We have the bridal suite."*

Rita pauses in the doorway as Mikal carries in their bags. She watches as he opens the window and lays the bags on the ground so as to save the bed for their more personal activities. She can tell he is nervous. Of course, neither of them has ever been in this situation before, but Rita's mind drifts to the previous day with Daniel and can't help but have preferred that this evening would have been with him rather than with this man who she doesn't know … but would soon know intimately.

Mikal asks, *"Would you like to wash up?"*

"Yes, please." With that, she leaves him and enters the bathroom.

There is plumbing inside this inn. That's another thing that makes it unique. She looks at herself in the mirror and wonders how many other brides have looked at themselves in this mirror before giving themselves to their new husbands. She examines all her features: Her eyes, hair, nose, and mouth. They will soon belong to someone else. And she cries.

In the bedroom, Mikal hears her crying. He hadn't expected it. He had thought through the day's events, and everything had gone according to plan, but he hadn't thought that his new wife would be crying. He moves to the door. He thinks about saying, *Is something wrong?* Before he can say anything, the door opens, and Rita comes out in her nightgown. The nightgown was a present from her mother, who told her that she had worn it on her first night with Rita's father.

Rita has wiped the tears from her eyes, and Mikal assumes that the reason she has been crying is that this will be her first time.

This is not Mikal's first time. There were two other women whom he had met and paid for when he was in Kyiv. That was just after Abraham and he had spoken for the first time about marriage to Rita. Mikal wanted to be experienced, and that was a practical way to achieve it.

Mikal waits near the bed as Rita crosses to him. He appreciates the significance of her mother's wedding nightgown and opens his arms to Rita as a welcoming gesture, a gesture that is meant to say, "Let's do this happily together. The first of many times."

She forces a smile, and they hug tentatively, awkwardly. Mikal leaves her and crosses to the bathroom, for it is now his turn to prepare.

As soon as he leaves her, Rita gets into bed and stares at the ceiling. How many brides had stared at this same ceiling before her?

In the bathroom Mikal looks in the mirror. He knows that Rita had just looked into this same mirror and had been crying. Mikal doesn't cry. That would be impractical, unmanly, and heard by his nervous bride.

Besides, there is no reason to cry. He puts on his nightshirt, bought for the occasion by his parents.

When he comes out, he is surprised that Rita is under the covers. She is surprised that he is in his nightshirt. She had never seen a man, other than her father, in a nightshirt.

Mikal says, *"I didn't expect you to be in bed already."*

Stoically she says, *"I am ready. Come to bed."*

He gets in bed beside her, and after straightening out the blanket over them, he kisses her. She realizes that she is about to make love to a man, and this—other than their kiss at the ceremony—is only the second time she has kissed him. She compares his kiss to that of Daniel and that forces her to cry again. She hadn't wanted to, but she couldn't help it.

"Is something wrong?"

"No." She turns to him and smiles.

She tries her best to be warm. He smiles back at her, and silently he removes his nightshirt.

And she, matter-of-factly and dutifully, pulls her nightgown off. She is now naked in front of a man for only the second time.

Mikal gets on top of her. She doesn't react. Sensing her reticence, Mikal thinks it must be the glare of the light, so he gets out of bed and crosses to the end table with its doilies and turns down the gaslight. He then turns and looks at her. She looks so small.

He crosses back to the bed, gets in beside her, and kisses her again.

She thinks about kiss number three. How many more kisses would be from this man in their lifetime together?

Mikal interrupts her thinking when he embraces her. The moment is at hand. Mikal is more self-conscious than Daniel had been.

How can she ever get through this? Then she knows. She'll think of Daniel, and it will be all right.

Suddenly, Mikal feels a change in Rita. She is warmer, more accepting. As they move from kissing to the more physical, Rita guides him, thinking all the time of Daniel. Mikal is excited by his bride's supposed eagerness for him. Rita is wet and ready for his penetration when she realizes that Mikal must believe that she is a virgin.

She braces herself and acts as a woman who has never made love before.

"Let me know if I am hurting you."

Rita winces convincingly. Then she cries and yelps as he enters her. She yelps to prove to her new husband that she is a virgin. She cries because she is not with Daniel.

*

Daniel is drunk when he enters his hovel of a house in Bukachivtski. He had stopped to drink at a tavern and stayed there until it closed. But while he was there, he was among other people. Now, he is alone with his thoughts of what Rita must be doing. It is almost too much to bear. He collapses on his bed and rolls over in grief. It is lucky for him that he quickly is unconscious, or he would be dwelling too much on the night that should have been his and Rita's.

*

In the inn near Berdichev, Mikal holds Rita, who is crying. He thinks it was because it was her first time, but her crying is because of her longing for Daniel.

Mikal says, *"It will be better after this. I promise."*

She allows herself to be comforted, but she doubts that what he says is true.

CHAPTER FOUR

The steamship companies were sending all their ships across the Atlantic to Europe, where they were loaded down with Russian Jews fleeing the oppression. They'd be crammed with the downtrodden human cargo and then make the crossing back. But then they would only stay in New York harbor long enough to unload the immigrants, pack their engine rooms with coal, and head out to the open sea to reach ports where more émigrés were huddled on the docks. Then this new group of huddled masses would pile onto the ships, where they'd wedge into inhuman conditions to brave the sea, the stifling conditions, and the foul odors while they prayed to find a better life than what they had left behind.

Entire villages disappeared from Earth as their inhabitants reached coastal city docks and boarded ships that sailed away for new, hopefully better, lives. Most were led to the lower steerage decks.

That's where Daniel found himself. Daniel scarcely knew anyone, but then again, he hardly knew anyone back in Russia. And Rita, the only person he cared about, wasn't with him … would never be with him. Perhaps it was better for him to begin a new life unburdened with a constant reminder of the end of his personal happiness.

As the ships are about to reach the new land, other passengers rush onto the deck when they hear some call out that they see the lady with the torch who greets them.

"It's her! It's the statue! It's America!"

Ships don't sail directly up to the pier in New York. All make the traditional and obligatory stop at Ellis Island, where passengers must register before they're allowed to enter America. Some are given showers, since the filth of their journey would turn the stomachs of the immigration authorities.

On his ship, the *Frisia*, Daniel was jammed in with the passengers in steerage. He is dirty; he is hungry, and he moves with the throng into the Great Hall.

In the Great Hall, six stations with seen-it-all immigration clerks are set up at the end of rows and rows of passengers. Few immigrants speak any English, and the clerks are hardly welcoming. These lowest-level bureaucrats are intimidating and officious. They look at the hordes facing them and wish for the unending lines to have an end. But that will never be since America is the dream in which all immigrants have been sold, a dream they hold on to. It is a dream that never ends.

Carrying only his fraying carpetbag, Daniel moves to the end of one of the lines. The line moves slowly, which gives Daniel plenty of time to study this large hall. It's a majestic building, the most majestic building he has ever seen. If this is what the buildings are like in America, it will have been worth the horrid conditions he underwent on the ship coming across the sea.

Daniel speaks to an old woman in line in front of him, but she doesn't respond. He tries again. Then he realizes she doesn't understand Russian. He tries in his broken English: "Hallo, friend."

She doesn't understand that either. She is a German who smiles at the friendly man who has tried to talk to her. He smiles back. Their corresponding smiles are his first communication in this new country. That said, he doesn't attempt to talk to her anymore, so the two strangers are content to move silently through the line.

Daniel looks ahead at some of the rest of the people in the line in front of him ... all kinds of people. Most are Russian like he is—like he was. Now he, and they, will be Americans.

Immigration clerk number three is all business when Daniel finally reaches the front of the line, and his German friend moves away. The woman is crying. Daniel doesn't know if they are tears of happiness or that there is some kind of problem for her. If it's a problem, he doesn't know enough English to help.

Before he can contemplate more, the clerk calls out, "Next!"

Daniel moves quickly. The clerk has a large notebook in which he writes the name of each of the persons who come before him.

Daniel says, "Hallo, friend."

The clerk isn't Daniel's friend. He doesn't want to be Daniel's friend. He just wants to do his work and go home. "Name?"

"Daniel Stabinski."

The clerk has been given the authorization to Americanize, or at least try to understand, what the applicants are saying.

He makes it simpler for Daniel. "Daniel Stabin."

Daniel resists the simplification. Daniel may not have much, but at least he has his own name. In his broken English: "I said 'Daniel Stabinski.' That is my name. Not Stabin. Stabinski."

The clerk looks up and sees the adamant young man in front of him. In reality, what Daniel calls himself makes no difference to the clerk. "Okay. Daniel Sabinski. Have it your way. Welcome to America."

The clerk stamps Daniel's papers, and Daniel passes through, ready for the challenge of his new life. As Daniel gives way to the next person in line and moves off, the clerk calls after him.

"Luggage and belongings at the end of the pier on the dock." Then the clerk turns back to the line in front of him: "Next."

Daniel smiles. The clerk had it wrong. Daniel has no luggage, no belongings. Everything he owns is in the carpet bag. Daniel leaves and then looks back to see the lines of people waiting to enter the Great Hall. He was one of them, but now he, for all intents and purposes, is an American, although he can only speak a few words of the language. He gets on the ferry that will take him to Battery Park in New York City and to his new life.

When the ferry docks, he is different from other immigrants. Many of them have come with other friends and family or have family greeting them with hugs and tears. Not Daniel, who walks quickly away from the pier.

When he looks into the city spreading out before him, he faces people, carts, buildings, and noise like he had never heard. *What is this?* Nothing had prepared him for the sheer energy of the exploding, burgeoning metropolis. And the city is not only filled with horses pulling wagons and carts, but primitive automobiles and a few buses share the roads. There are more people in the block he is facing than in all Bukachivtsi. It is at once overwhelming and heady. As he is magnetically drawn toward his new life, he passes the German woman who had been in line in front of him in the Great Hall. She is surrounded by people who have met her at the dock. She looks up at Daniel, and they exchange glances. She is smiling again. He smiles, too, but his smile is a smile of determination.

As Daniel enters his new world, he doesn't have a particular place to go, but on some level, he likes it that way.

The *Dania* docked at Ellis Island a week after Daniel's ship arrived in New York. For Rita, it is an entirely different experience than the one Daniel had. Mikal has enough money to have paid for rooms on the upper decks for his whole family. This was a family Rita had never met before the ocean voyage to America, but these people would become the center of her life in her new country.

Rita's father and mother are there as well. Privileged, Rita and the passengers from the upper decks move off first. As they move down the gangplank, they pass the faces looking up at them from those in steerage, pleading faces who have always known their place. These faces also have dreams, but they were poor in their homelands, and they can only envision being poor in this new land. This is how Daniel traveled when he came to America.

They arrive in the Great Hall. Mikal has assumed leadership of the Gleisserman family. His elderly father had always been in charge, but the enormity of the move to this country is something that had to be left to the next generation. It is a right-of-passage for Mikal that has come with their passage somewhere across the Atlantic.

Mikal keeps them all together as they enter the line leading to the clerks. Try as they will to stay together, the horde of debarking immigrants has momentarily separated the Gleissermans from one another. Going to one line is Rita's mother, who carries a small cedar box from their home in Russia.

When he sees what is happening, Mikal shouts in Russian to his family above the din, *"If we can't be together now, let us meet just outside the building—in America!*

Unable to stay together, they are swept in different directions. In front of the same immigration clerk who had naturalized Daniel is a scared elderly woman in a babushka. She is so nervous that she shakes, not an uncommon emotion that the immigration clerks see on an hourly basis. Behind this woman is one of Rita's new in-laws, who witnesses the exchange between the coldhearted immigration clerk and the terrified woman.

"Name?"

The woman is so rattled that she can't remember what her family told her to say. All had agreed to say one last name, but in her fear, she had forgotten how to say that name in English.

She mutters in Yiddish, *"Fergusson,"* which means "I forgot."

He writes what he assumes to be her name on the ledger: "Ferguson."

From now on, that shaken woman will be known as Hannah Ferguson.

As his brothers and family members disperse to the various immigration stations, Mikal does his best to supervise. He hands them slips of paper with addresses, but that is all he can do as they are swept away by the flood of people in the hall. There are too many people crowding in too many lanes. He looks on in frustration.

One of his brothers works his way to the front of immigration clerk number two.

The clerk says, "Name?"

His youngest brother says, "Gleisserman."

The clerk says, "Gleiss," writes it down, and then stamps the paper. "Welcome to America, Mr. Gleiss."

With his new name, he walks off.

In front of yet another clerk is yet another brother.

That clerk says, "What's your name? I need your name."

That brother says, "Gleisserman."

That clerk says, "Glasserman it is."

And that clerk stamps the paper. The brother walks off, hearing, "Next."

At immigration clerk number six, Mikal and Rita stand together. The clerk assumes that they are married and points to them.

Mikal answers, "Mikal and Rita Gleisserman."

The clerk has hardly listened. It's lucky he has heard their first names accurately, but he says, "Mikal and Rita Glass."

Before Mikal or Rita can object, the clerk stamps their papers and says, "Next."

Not knowing what else to do, the two leave the immigration clerk and enter America with a new last name—and a different last name than either of Mikal's brothers. Definitely only in America.

CHAPTER FIVE

Hyman Greenbaum always opens his delicatessen at exactly seven in the morning by rolling up the awning/window covering on Houston Street on the lower East Side. He follows the same pattern even when it's raining or snowing. There is often a line of customers since his food is considered the best in the area where most of the Russian Jewish immigrants have settled. Today, it's a downpour, and the awning opens to reveal only one customer. Actually, it's not a customer. It's Daniel, who would be a customer if he had any money.

Greenbaum opens the door and lets Daniel come out of the weather. Greenbaum looks at the drenched Daniel and recognizes him. "You have been out there before. I have seen you."

Daniel says that he heard that Greenbaum's Deli was the best.

Greenbaum looks at the drenched Daniel. "You want corned beef? I'll put some on rye."

Daniel shakes his head no.

"You don't want my corned beef?"

In his awkward attempt at English, "I want food. I just can't pay for food."

There is something about Daniel that strikes Hyman Greenbaum's heart. Daniel reminds him of his son Leon who passed away from tuberculosis two years ago. Leon would be Daniel's age now.

"On me. My treat. Come."

Without any more being said, the deli owner goes behind the counter and takes out a slab of corned beef as Daniel trails after. The owner expertly slices the meat and then takes two pieces of rye bread and slaps down the corned beef between them. Putting the sandwich on a plate, he hands it to Daniel.

"You want mustard?"

"Yes, please."

Greenbaum hands Daniel a jar of mustard and a knife, which Daniel uses to slather the mustard on the sandwich. Greenbaum watches Daniel eagerly take huge bites that consume the sandwich in less than a minute.

"How long has it been since you ate?"

Daniel says, "Tuesday. I ate food on Tuesday."

Greenbaum says, "Today is Thursday."

Without saying another word, Greenbaum goes to fetch a push broom from the small closet behind the counter. Hyman looks at the young man in front of him. There is something about him.

"You are like my son Leon."

Greenbaum hands Daniel the broom. "Now you've got job and food. And I guess you don't have place to stay, or you wouldn't be out in rain like wet dog."

Daniel is so grateful. He takes the broom. "Thank you to you."

"The small room in back. You can stay there. I won't pay you. Not yet. Not until I see if you are good worker. You get place to sleep and best corned beef in city."

Daniel can only say, "Thank you, thank you, friend."

Greenbaum watches Daniel go about sweeping. Greenbaum knows immediately that he has done the right thing—for Daniel and for himself.

*

Though still in the Russian Jewish section, the Glass/Glasserman/ Gleiss horde of husbands and wives and children have found housing much easier than Daniel has. Mikal's brother Josef, with his wife, Goldie, and their daughter, Rivka, move along crowded Orchard Street. Nobody who lives on Orchard Street ever considers the irony that there are not any orchards close to this street. Just tenements growing like orchards.

Josef pushes a cart with their belongings while Goldie has the slip of paper in her hand with an address. Around them on both sides of the street are people just like them. And one or two groups are also seeking the places where they will live. All the tenements are pretty much the same, but one will be different for Josef and his family. That one will be their home. They pause in front of the one on the address. All look up.

Rivka says to her parents, *"Can I go in first?"*

A look between Josef and Goldie. *Why not?*

Goldie says to her daughter, *"Go ahead. Our home will be on the third floor."*

Rivka excitedly enters the building. Josef and Goldie trail after. Josef takes Goldie's hand as they move into the building. Inside, it is dark. Even the stairway up to the third floor is dark. When they reach the third floor, they find Rivka waiting.

Rivka asks, *"Which one is ours?"*

Josef takes the key that he was given and moves to apartment 2. He opens the door, and Rivka darts in front of her mother and father. They move in after her. To other people, the place would be dismal, but considering where they had lived in Russia, this cramped apartment is practically a palace. As she whirls around in the kitchen, which has a bathtub in the middle of it, she exclaims, "I love it!"

Josef turns to Goldie, *"Our new home."*

As if to punctuate, he puts down his bags and turns to Goldie. *"We have Mikal to thank."*

Goldie mouths, *"Thank you, Mikal."*

All around Orchard Street and on all the streets surrounding, husbands and wives and families enter similar tenements. They carry bags of clothes and essentials. They enter with mixed emotions of relief, wonderment, and curiosity. Few had lived in a building with more than one story. Few had buildings with gas lamps. Adjustments have to be made, but they all knew that when they fled their homelands. They even have difficulty communicating with each other since some speak German; others speak Russian, Dutch, or Hebrew. Eventually, Yiddish will become their common language.

In another apartment in another tenement, Mikal's other brother—now Sid Glasserman—and his wife, Sadie, and their two children Shem and Leah stand in the main room that is nearly identical to the one where Josef and his family now live. Mikal and Rita stand back and watch Shem and Leah move around the new home. Mikal hands Sid a key. Apparently, the generous Mikal has been the provider for his entire family and says, *"Live and be well."*

Josef, the stoic one in the family, hides his gratitude and emotion and puts his arms around his children, then his wife, as he takes the key. *"I owe you, Mikal."*

Mikal says, *"No, you don't. We're family."*

Rita has watched the interchange between the two brothers and appreciates what a good man she has been given to marry. They leave Josef and Sadie and their family to settle into their new lives.

Now, on a different street in a more affluent neighborhood, Rita walks with Mikal. She looks up at the tall buildings in wonderment. Where will their home be? Rita walks ahead. Mikal knows that she has passed the building where they will live and stops. Rita finally realizes that Mikal is not by her side, and she darts back to him. She points to the building where Mikal waits. She points. Mikal nods and asks her, *"If you don't like it, tell me, and we'll find someplace else."*

"Can we go inside?"

Mikal smiles and kids her: *"No. We'll just live here on the street."*

He offers her his hand, and they walk up the stairs and into the door of the building. Inside, it is almost luxury compared to the tenements where his brothers and their families live. Even the stairway has more light than the buildings on Orchard Street. He stops on the second floor and uses his key to open the door for them. Before he lets her cross the threshold, he says, *"Close your eyes."*

They stop in the doorway.

"Now open."

She does. Rita looks around in surprise. There are clearly lots more rooms, all furnished in good taste. How can this be? She races around the apartment. She pauses at the couch, the dining room table, runs into the bedroom, and sees the double bed with its handknitted comforter. Everything is in place. He follows her in. She goes to him, and in a mixture of gratitude and amazement, says, *"Mikal?"*

He says, *"What can I say? Your father chose the right brother for you."*

He then goes on to explain that his sister, Miriam, came last year. She picked out this home, the furniture. *"She and I think alike ... except the lamps. I told her exactly what I wanted."*

"I love it all—especially the lamps." She kisses him, and they embrace, looking at their place.

She says, *"You have to tell me how we have such a fine place."*

Mikal has been keeping his wealth a secret. Now he opens up: *"Before I left Berdichev, I sold my store."*

He then takes out his leather purse and pours a torrent of diamonds onto the bedspread. She can't believe how many. Mikal tells her, *"It was a big store."*

He then scoops almost all the rest of the diamonds in his hand and displays them to her. *"These are for my new store. My new American store."*

Somehow, Mikal's wealth and kindness make her life with him passable, even though she hides that much of her heart remains with Daniel. She hugs Mikal, as if to hug away the hurt of her continuing separation from Daniel.

CHAPTER SIX

It's early morning, and Hyman finishes opening up Greenbaum's Delicatessen when his wife, Rose, enters from the street. Rose is not an attractive woman, but she is dedicated to her husband, and that is enough for him. She is the one who picks up their fresh vegetables and meats from the vendors. They bake their breads and bagels in the rear of the store and restaurant. Greenbaum's Delicatessen has always been run by the two of them, and they had fully intended to turn over their business to their son, Leon, when that time came. That time never came. Now, it is as much the family income as it is to keep their minds off their loss.

Hyman helps his wife unpack the boxes on the workspace behind the counter. She moves through to the back. Hyman starts to put the meats away when he hears a shriek from the rear! She comes running in. "I saw a ghost! It's Leon's ghost! Asleep in the room back there!

Those who come from the old country are filled with superstitions and beliefs in ghosts and spirits. Hyman embraces his terrified wife. He knows what she saw. As Hyman holds Rose, Daniel rubs the sleep from his eyes and enters from the rear.

Hyman says, "My Yiddisha mama, it's not Leon. It's not a ghost. It's Daniel. Say hello to Daniel."

Rose now scrutinizes Daniel. She is both reassured and disappointed. She asks, "So who is this Daniel?"

Daniel answers for himself in his still incipient English. "Your kind husband gives me a place to stay."

Hyman jumps in. "But not for free. He will work here."

Rose pulls Hyman aside as Daniel moves to put away the vegetables and meats. Rose sees this and is pleased with Daniel's contribution. Rose says, "He is so much like Leon. He's as thoughtful as Leon."

"What can it hurt? He needs a place. We all need a place."

Rose agrees and repeats, "What can it hurt?"

Then Hyman asks Daniel, "Have you finished sweeping up?"

"Yes."

Hyman hands Daniel a large, sharp knife. "See this corned beef?"

"Yes."

"Take this knife and cut third off and put it in the one pan marked 'lean.' Take another for pan marked 'leanest.' And the rest in pan marked just 'corned beef.'"

"But it's all the same corned beef."

"If I can't tell, they can't tell. What can I say? Some customers just like to pay more."

Daniel smiles at the Greenbaum acumen and goes about his appointed task.

*

Mikal and Rita walk along Houston Street. Whereas many of the streets in lower Manhattan are filled with pushcarts and stands selling any matter of goods and foods, this street has already evolved into storefronts. Rita has never window-shopped in her life since there were hardly any windows of any kind in Bukachivtski. As she passes the stores, she loves looking at the dresses in the windows, and Mikal enjoys her enjoyment. They pass a furniture maker, then a shoemaker who works on stretching and pounding leather in the window, and then a furrier. The next store is New World Lights and Lamps. Rita looks in the window and moves off to see what other stores might be down the block. Mikal waits until Rita realizes he isn't walking next to her. That has become Mikal's way when he has a surprise.

She comes back to him. *"Why are we stopping here?"*

Mikal says, *"If I told you, it wouldn't be a surprise."*

With that, he takes out a key and unlocks the door. They enter. With great ceremony, Mikal turns on the light switch. Like a fairy land, all the lights and lamps spring to life. Enchanted, Rita walks in and around the various lamps and fixtures and is overwhelmed by the gleaming, glittering display. Indeed, the world is making its transition from gas lamps to electric ones. Mikal delights in her enthusiasm and watches as her face turns to one of practicality. Rita catches her breath enough to ask, *"But what do you know about lights?"*

Mikal smiles. *"In our shtetls, there were not many lights. America is a new land of lights. Lights and lamps that everybody wants. What I know is business. If you have what people want, that's a business."*

Rita admires Mikal's business sense. *"Then you own this store?"*

They embrace as he continues his explanation. *"It was the biggest store I could afford with the diamonds I had. Look around. These are only the store samples. People look, and then we bring them their lamps in crates in boxes from the back warehouse."*

With all the excitement, Rita suddenly feels faint. *"You say this store has everything?"*

"More than everything."

"Then does this store have a bathroom?"

Pointing proudly: *"Second door on the left."*

As she moves off, Mikal sees that his wife had gone pale. He calls after her, *"Are you all right?"*

From inside the bathroom, *"I feel a little sick."*

Mikal cannot do anything for his wife. He paces, and then he goes to the front door of the store and places an "open" sign in the window.

CHAPTER SEVEN

Daniel stood looking at the room where he had been living for half a year. He had turned it into a comfortable place for himself, but the time had come for him to move on. He picks up the carpet bag and now has another suitcase as well. He grabs the treasured photo of himself and Rita and manages to squeeze it into the carpet bag.

Rose comes up behind him. "Remember when I thought you were a ghost?"

He laughs. She laughs. And then he turns and embraces Rose. In the months he has been working and living here, she has become his surrogate mother.

Rose says, "And now the ghost is leaving."

Hyman enters. Rose says, "Hyman, tell him he can't go. Offer him more money."

"Rose, we can't hold Daniel back."

Rose breaks down. "I don't want this. I don't want this!"

Daniel faces them both. All their eyes are filled with tears. Daniel's English is much improved: "When I came to America, I had nothing. You gave me something. You gave me home. You made me believe I could be somebody. I will never forget your kindness. I go now, but part of me will always be behind the counter out there. I lost my mother and father long ago back in Ukraine. I had to come here to find another mother and father."

They all hug each other; none wants to be the first to let go.

Hyman releases first. "Go, son. Proud you should make us."

Rose adds, "Come. Take some food." Rose pulls him into the counter area and takes a box and begins putting in corned beef, rye bread, and coleslaw. Hyman grabs a ladle and finds soup simmering on the stove. He ladles some into a container and adds it to the box.

Rose says, "You know where we are if you need more."

"I know."

Hyman says, "Let him go."

Rose says, "I can't."

Hyman says, "We have to. It's best for him. We have to do what's best for him."

One more anguished hug from Rose, and Daniel moves to the door. He manages to carry his carpet bag, his suitcase, and the box of food. As he does, he passes a well-to-do gentleman who sees Daniel carrying the box of food.

The gentleman asks, "Is the food good here?"

"The best. Get the leanest corned beef. Costs more, but worth every penny."

With that, Daniel walks out of the delicatessen.

*

On a hill overlooking the campus of NYU in the heights, two college freshmen throw a baseball back and forth. They have baseball gloves. One of the young men is Ellman, but he has always hated his name. He comes from Hoboken across the river, so everyone calls him Hoby, which is all he answers to. On the finger of his throwing hand, he sports a distinctive ring that his father gave him when he got accepted into college. He was the first in his family to graduate high school.

The other is the Irish American Pat. Pat has a trace of the brogue, but since he was born in this country, it's only a trace. The two have roomed together for a year, and they think pretty much the same about everything by now and are simpatico about sports, women, and their futures. That is why, when they decided to bring in a new roommate to defray their expenses, they are concerned that this new person will upset their dynamic. And all they know about him is his name: Stabinakoff or Stabinski or Stabin-something or other. They throw the ball back and forth harder and harder, as if to amplify their concern.

Pat says, "It was your idea."

Hoby counters, "But that doesn't mean it was right. You know I don't know what I'm doing."

Pat says, "Maybe this guy Daniel will be an okay Joe."

Hoby throws back the ball even harder and says, "And if he ain't?"

Pat says, "You should have thought of that before."

Hoby says, "We needed the money for the rent after Gordon moved out. It was a way. C'mon. May as well go see about this guy."

A throw or two more before they go back down the hill to the college and move toward a dorm building. When they enter their tiny room, there are three single beds and hardly any room to turn around. Their two beds are already spoken for. The other bed has its thin mattress rolled up.

Hoby says, "He still ain't here."

Pat offers, "All we know about him is that he had to be smart enough to get into this school."

The door opens. With some trepidation, both look to see what this Daniel is like. Daniel carries in his suitcase, his carpet bag, and his box of food from the deli.

Daniel, "Is this my room?"

Hoby says, "It is if you're Daniel."

Daniel says, "That is who I am. Hallo, friends. And since this is our room, this food is for all of us."

Daniel presents the box and opens the top. As the aroma wafts upward, the perpetually hungry Hoby attacks the food. Hoby says to Pat, "What were we worried about? I like this guy already. Corned beef, bagels. Jew food! I love Jew food! Here!"

Hoby tosses a bagel to Pat, who catches it in the baseball glove he hadn't taken off. As they all scarf down food, Pat says, "I'm Pat Reardon."

Hoby, with his mouth full and corned beef dripping out, says, "I'm Ellman Vitarelli, but everybody calls me Hoby. In fact, if you call me Ellman, I won't even turn around."

Daniel says, "Why do they call you Hoby?"

Pat straightens him out. "They call him Hoby because he comes from Hoboken."

Daniel says, "Okay, Hoby." Daniel starts to unload his belongings. Hoby and Pat help as they continue to eat the food that Daniel has brought in.

Hoby wants to find out as much as they can about their new roommate. "Where are you from, anyway?

"Bukachivtski."

They just stare at him. No way could they pronounce that. Daniel clarifies. "Near Kaminovka." Not any clearer. He finally says, "It is Ukraine."

Pat says, "That's Russia?"

Daniel shrugs. He realizes to people in America anyplace near Russia is Russia.

Pat says, "They say you did really good on the college entrance test."

"I study hard. When you work hard, good things come."

Daniel now takes out his cherished photograph of Rita and himself. It is the only physical thing he has left of his relationship with her. With some reverence, he puts it on a dresser. Hoby picks up the picture and sees how pretty Rita is. Impressed, he asks, "Is this your girlfriend?"

Daniel will be open to talking about almost anything with his new friends, but Rita is not something he wants to talk about. Not yet anyway. He can only say, "That is Rita and me. Please put the picture down."

Immediately, they can tell this is a sore spot for their new roommate.

Hoby says, "You're gonna be staying here with us. You're going to tell us the story sooner or later."

Daniel sighs and looks at Rita and him in the photograph. "Much later."

*

In the Queens, New York, neighborhood of Ridgewood is the Linden Hills Jewish Cemetery. Most of it is empty of graves and headstones as the Jewish community is still relatively new. As time goes by, more and more of the rolling hills will have the gravesites of those who have come to America where they have ended their journeys.

Sadly, Linden Hills is the place of one of the first events that Rita and Mikal and their large family are attending together. Though Rita's father had been the one to force Rita to become Mikal's wife in an arranged marriage, he had done what he felt was best for her. She has tried to move past that, and the good man that Mikal is makes that somewhat easier for her. She stands between her husband and her disconsolate mother as the mourners surround the coffin.

At the graveside, Mikal's brothers and their families have joined in support. Rita's mother has aged because of the experience of watching her husband die. She leans on Rita both physically and emotionally. Rita's black dress blossoms outward since Rita is now visibly pregnant.

Bearded Rabbi Horowitz leads the final prayer for Abraham, which is the traditional "Mourner's Kaddish."

"Yitgadal v'yitkadash sh'mei raba. B'alma di v'ra chirutei, v'yamlich malchutei, b'chayeichon uv'yomeichon uv'chayei d'chol beit Yisrael, baagala uviz'man kariv. V'im'ru: Amen. Y'hei sh'mei raba m'varach l'alam ul'almei almaya."

The sobbing from Rita and her mother echoes as the cemetery workers lower the casket into the open grave before each of them takes a shovelful of dirt and places it on the coffin. This is a tradition, but one that is difficult for all since it signifies finality.

*

In the middle of today's lesson, the veteran professor Jonathan Wineglass faces his forty students as he always does. He has hope that what he offers will get through, though he knows all the young men have to take his class in American history before they move into their specialties. He was that way himself, until one day, in a college class long ago, he realized his specialty is American history.

Among those at desks are Daniel, Hoby, and Pat. Unlike Hoby and Pat, Daniel not only reads the assigned text, but he also absorbs what he reads and stores it away in his brain.

Professor Wineglass asks the class, "From your reading of the textbook, what else is significant about Benjamin Harrison's administration?"

None of the students raises his hand. Finally, Daniel, though not wishing to appear to be the class know-it-all, raises his hand.

The professor checks the seating chart. "Mr. Stabinski."

Daniel answers, "Benjamin Harrison was the grandson of William Henry Harrison, and his term was between the two terms of Grover Cleveland."

"Yes, that is who he is, but what were his accomplishments? Sadly or not, people are only measured by what they do, not by who they are."

The professor is surprised when Daniel feels challenged and decides to offer up a small but concise history of the Benjamin Harrison presidential term of office. "President Benjamin Harrison signed the McKinley Tariff Bill into law and was a supporter of the 1890 Sherman Silver Purchase Act as well as signing the Sherman Anti-Trust Act into law. He advocated for forest reserves, endorsed two bills designed to prevent southern states from denying the vote to Negroes, and appointed Frederick Douglas ambassador to Haiti. He convened the first Pan-American Conference in 1889 and was the first to propose building a canal across Central America."

Hoby, Pat, the class, and the professor are duly impressed with how much Daniel has retained from his reading. Professor Wineglass turns to the others in the class. "Everybody, pay attention. Mr. Stabinski is not even an American."

Hoby whispers to Pat, "Where did he learn all that?"

Pat whispers back, "In the book we should have read but Daniel did."

*

The New York-Presbyterian Hospital was founded in the mid 1800s. Though Mikal and his family are far from Presbyterian, Mikal insisted that his and Rita's child should be born in a hospital whatever its denomination. In the old country, children were born at home. This was a custom, plus the fact that the only hospitals were in cities far, far away.

Mikal is not alone in the waiting room. His entire family, along with Rita's mother, are gathered around him while Rita is attended to by the doctor in the obstetrics ward. Other expectant fathers wait along with Mikal. Many fathers speak many languages, but all with similar fears and expectations. Though it isn't hot, some sweat; some smoke to alleviate their tension.

Mikal shares a moment with Rita's mother, Esther. Though they had hardly known each other, the dramatic events that brought them to this point—the marriage to Rita, coming to America, and the death of her husband, Abraham—have brought these two closer. Mikal takes her hand and says quietly, *This is our first of your grandchildren. The first of many, I hope.*

"My Abraham would have been happy."

Mikal indicates toward heaven, *"He is. I know it."*

They hug.

Mikal looks toward his brothers. Josef comes to him. Mikal asks him, *"Were you this nervous when your first was born?"*

Josef laughs. *"Who knew to be nervous? I was bringing in the crops to market that day. I got home a week later, and the family had grown without me being nervous."*

Inside the delivery room, a doctor and a midwife huddle around Rita, who grimaces and grits her teeth with the pain of childbirth. The doctor has brought many children into the world. And since New York City is filled with immigrants, he and the midwife are used to hearing a lot of mothers talking and screaming in languages they can't identify. The midwife checks the dilation. "I can see the baby, missus."

Rita grimaces and is barely able to get out, *"When will the hurting stop?!"*

The sympathetic doctor hears her and says, "I don't understand what you're asking, but you can keep talking and yell out in any language if you want."

The midwife joins in, "Help us, Mrs. Glass. Help your baby come into the world."

Rita doesn't understand what they are saying to her, but she appreciates their sympathetic tone. One more push, and as Rita screams, the baby comes out into the hands of the waiting doctor.

The midwife moves to Rita's ear and whispers, "You have a son."

Rita cries in happiness.

In the waiting room, all the other men have left. The smoke from their cigarettes has gone with them. Just Mikal and his brothers and their wives are there when the doctor enters with the news. The doctor doesn't know which of the men is Rita's husband. He questions, "Mr. Glass?" Mikal's brothers push Mikal toward the Christian doctor, who is happy to say, "Mr. Glass, you have a son." He mispronounces, "Matzo tov, right?"

Mikal loves to be able to say, *"An American son."*

The women beam as Mikal's brothers all pound him on the back.

CHAPTER EIGHT

The three friends have grown inseparable. This is a truly unique relationship for Daniel since—other than Rita—there had never been anybody who is a contemporary with whom he could share his most personal thoughts. They take a break from studying; rather, Daniel takes a break from studying. Pat and Hoby are usually on a break. Pat and Hoby constantly tell him that "even geniuses need to get some time away."

They escort/drag Daniel to Pete's Tavern, a roadhouse that serves workers and students alike. Covering most walls is risqué artwork that Hoby loves, Pat likes, and Daniel tolerates. All three sit at the bar and order drinks from Pete, the owner/bartender whom Hoby and Pat know, and Daniel is only just meeting.

Hoby says, "Pete, I'll have a whiskey.

Pat says, "Make that two, Pete.

Pete looks at Daniel on the other stool. Daniel is torn. He usually doesn't drink, but he wants to be one of the boys and finally blurts out, "I'll have a vodka, friend."

As Pete puts a glass in front of each of them, he comments to Daniel, "Everyone calls me Pete, but I guess 'friend' will do."

Pete pours a whiskey for Hoby and Pat and pours a vodka for Daniel.

Pat says, "This round will be on me."

Daniel says, "I'll pay for the next round. I have money saved up from when I worked at the delicatessen."

Pat stops Daniel from getting the bartender's attention. Pat tells Daniel, "No, this round is on me. Your round will be when you tell us about Rita."

They have another round at the bar. Daniel is not used to drinking and gets drunk quickly. He fairly falls off the stool, but Hoby catches him before he hits the floor. Pat turns to Hoby as he holds Daniel erect. "Let's get him to a table. If he drops from a chair, he'll have a shorter way to fall."

Pat and Hoby almost must carry their drunken friend to a table at the rear of Pete's Tavern. Hoby darts back to the bar to retrieve the bottles of whiskey and vodka and glasses as Pete organizes Daniel into a chair.

When Hoby returns and puts the bottles and glasses on the table, Pat turns to Daniel. "Okay, friend; it's Rita time.

Hoby is complicit: "Come on, Danny. Let's hear it."

Even drunk, Daniel is not ready. "No."

Hoby has always been one to share his conquests or defeats. "Hey. I told you about Geraldine and the empty boxcar."

Pat remembers the story all too well and chimes in like a train: "Woo! Woo!"

Hoby fesses up, "That's what she sounded like. What can I say?"

Both look at the drunken Daniel. Pat says, "Now, about your girlfriend, Rita?"

Daniel sees that only true friends would be as supportive as they are. Maybe he needed the alcohol to loosen his tongue. At any rate, he is ready to tell them what happened between him and the love of his life. "Rita is not my girlfriend. She was my girlfriend. Then she got married."

Hoby is immediately sympathetic. "Women ... they don't know when they got something good."

Daniel is now in tears. "She loves me. I know that. She wanted to marry me, but they told her she had to marry somebody else."

Hoby is less sophisticated than Pat. "What? Nobody tells people who they have to marry."

Pat has heard about arranged marriages. "They do in some countries. I heard about it."

Pat turns sympathetically to Daniel. "Is that what happened?"

Daniel is drained. "Yes, but she still loves me."

Hoby asks him, "Are you going to try to get her back?"

Daniel yells so loudly that the rest of the patrons of Pete's look over when he exclaims: "Don't you understand? I don't know where she is!"

Pete stops pouring a drink at the bar for one of his regulars and looks toward the weeping Daniel, who repeats forlornly, "I don't know where she is."

Pat says softly to Daniel, "If you did know, would you try to find her?"

Daniel can't answer. He just cries.

*

In his new home, baby Nathan is crying too. But that's what babies do. Mikal and Rita carry their newborn home in a blanket and bring him into the house and then the room that they have prepared for him. This new person will soon become the center of their world. Rita has spent the last few months getting the nursery ready for him. She hopes he'll like it, but for the moment, all he does is cry about it.

Rita says to her newborn, *"Oh, no. I was hoping you'd like it."*

Mikal smiles and addresses the baby. *"This is your room, Nathan."*

Rita looks at the baby while talking to Mikal. *"Nathan. Named after your father, Noah."*

The Jewish tradition asks that babies be named with the first initial of a deceased relative. In that way, the person can live on through a new life.

Mikal says, *"Some traditions are good."*

Rita could have named their son after her own father, but she never quite forgave Abraham for forcing her to marry Mikal. Mikal is a good man, a good provider, and no doubt will be a good father for their son; but still, she has a regret about Daniel that will never go away.

Rita lays Nathan down in his crib. They stand and admire their complete family unit. In the language that they have always spoken, Mikal says to Rita, *"I have made a decision: Since Nathan is born as an American, he should speak English. And the best way for him to learn English is for us to speak English so he will hear it in his home. I will begin:* 'Good morning, my wife, Rita.'"

Rita laughs and says in Russian, *"You don't sound like Mikal."*

Mikal says in Russian, *"We must do this."* Then, in English, he says to her, "You say, 'Good morning, my husband, Mikal.'"

Rita stumbles, but she does her best: "Good morning, my husband, Mikal."

*

The graduation exercises for the college class of 1908 are held in one of the large lecture halls. All of the graduates are in caps and gowns, and friends and relatives attend. Since Daniel doesn't have any relatives, he asked Hyman and Rose to be there for him. When he brought the invitation to the deli, Rose cried. Then they closed on graduation day so they could be there for Daniel.

What makes the graduation memorable is the speaker who gives a commencement address. President Theodore Roosevelt looks smaller in person, but he is such a large personality he overshadows everyone on the platform. President Roosevelt has a special affinity for New York City, having been a police commissioner there and governor of New York State.

The college president, with a huge beard that comes halfway down the front of his gown, does the honors of welcoming the graduates and their relatives and friends. In truth, while he is speaking, all eyes are on President Roosevelt. Would Roosevelt be that captivating if he weren't president? Nobody can say, but he is magnetic.

Hyman and Rose can't believe it. They are there to see Daniel graduate, and they get to see a real president of the United States. This is a story they are bound to tell for years to come.

The college president says what he is supposed to say: "It is my pleasure to introduce the valedictorian for the class of 1908 …"

In the audience, along with Hoby and Pat's parents and numerous other relatives, is a young woman, Edith. Edith is bursting with pride. For the moment, it is unclear who she is there to celebrate, but when the college president introduces "Daniel Stabinski" to speak and he crosses the stage, Edith smiles so broadly, it would be clear to anyone seeing her that she and Daniel Stabinski have a relationship. Edith sits next to Hyman and Rose, for they are the ones who introduced her to Daniel. She is the niece of one of their customers, and Rose liked her immediately as one who would be right for Daniel. She arranged for him to come by on a Tuesday evening when she knew that Edith would be at Greenbaum's Deli with her aunt and uncle. Sparks flew, and Daniel left the deli with some bagels—and with Edith. Things progressed from there, and she and Daniel became a twosome.

Daniel pauses on his way to the podium to shake hands with Hoby and Pat, and he nods to Edith, Hyman, and Rose in the audience. He also pauses to shake hands with the college president and then President Roosevelt. Even though Daniel's mind is on the speech he is about to give, the idea of Daniel Stabinski from Bukachivtski in the Ukraine sharing a stage with the president of the United States is overwhelming for him. Daniel's English has improved to the point that, other than an occasional word here or there, some people might think he had been born in this country.

"Ladies and gentlemen, fellow graduates, faculty, friends, and President Roosevelt, it is an honor for me to address everyone today. It is particularly emotional for me since I am not from this country, yet I have been welcomed with the open arms of America ... so welcoming that I find myself talking to such a distinguished audience including the president of the United States."

President Roosevelt nods and smiles and tries not to take too much attention away from Daniel—though that is a failed mission, for Roosevelt is far too charismatic.

Daniel continues, "This is truly the land of opportunity. Fellow graduates, the world is indeed now open to us—all of us—at the beginning of this new century. Who knows what will unfold in the next hundred years? But we can all be assured there will be advances in science and medicine and social progress in areas and fields we have not yet even imagined. We should all breathe in the next century and fill our lungs with tomorrow."

Roosevelt thinks about what Daniel has said and loves the image and even contemplates borrowing those words for some future speech he might give.

Hyman and Rose, besides being impressed with what Daniel is saying, are not used to him speaking English so well. Pat and Hoby always knew he had it in him, and Edith is spellbound.

Daniel continues: "From up here, the air is magnificent. We have come so far so fast, and we must now promise to dedicate ourselves to our responsibility, a responsibility built for us by all those who have preceded us and worked so hard and sacrificed to make this country a great nation. We are now in a position to lead the world and to point the way toward the future, since we graduates are indeed the future. Let us welcome that tomorrow with the same kind of spirit that has brought us to where we are today. Thank you."

The crowd applauds enthusiastically. Daniel moves to take his seat. On the way there, he passes President Roosevelt, who shakes Daniel's hand. That moment will never be lost on Daniel. Roosevelt whispers in Daniel's ear, "Bully."

Daniel sits between Pat and Hoby among the graduates. Hoby slaps Daniel on the back. Pat is more restrained, but in his mind, he is slapping Daniel on the back as well.

President Roosevelt opens his folded papers to begin his speech but first acknowledges Daniel and Daniel's remarks. "Wasn't that bully?"

The crowd applauds again. They couldn't agree more.

CHAPTER NINE

In the small park near her home, Rita watches four-year-old Nathan playing with David, another four-year-old. The boys didn't know each other until five minutes ago, but that doesn't stop them from believing instantaneously that they are best friends. Children can do that. Amused at the immediate affection between their two sons are Rita, and David's mother, Ruth. For a few minutes, the two women don't speak to each other. They just enjoy the growing relationship between their sons. When both boys start climbing adjacent slides, the women are more concerned. Simultaneously, they yell, "Be careful!" Then they laugh at how simpatico they, themselves, have become as well.

The gregarious Ruth smiles and says to Rita, "I'm from Lithuania."

Rita smiles back and says, "The Ukraine."

"I'm Ruth Messirow."

"I'm Rita Glass."

Ruth and Rita watch for only a second or two more before Ruth says, "And now we find ourselves here. A world away."

They look at their sons again, and Ruth sees David about to pour a bucket of sand over Nathan's head before she shouts a warning, "David! Don't do that!"

The boys freeze.

Nathan yells back, "I wanted him to!"

Rita and Ruth laugh. Ruth asks, "What is your son's name?

"Nathan."

"My boy is David. They get along." Ruth studies Nathan's face. "He has such beautiful blue eyes."

"Thank you. There's a kindness to your David.

"Thank you, Rita."

Ruth asks, "Do you and your Nathan come here often?"

Rita knows why Ruth is asking. "Tuesdays and Thursdays." Rita is glad they have made a connection and adds, "I can come here on those days."

Ruth smiles and says, "I would like that."

They turn back to watching their sons continue to get along. Game after game, Nathan and David chase, wrestle, and laugh.

As is his usual pattern, Mikal comes from work this way. This time he stops to see what his wife and a woman are watching. After kissing his wife and nodding to Ruth, Mikal says to Rita, "It looks like our son has made a friend."

Rita says, "His name is David. And this is David's mother, Ruth."

Mikal says, "Nice to meet you. I am Mikal, Rita's husband and Nathan's father.

Ruth says, "Good to meet your family."

Nathan stops playing with David long enough to look up and see Mikal talking to his mother and Ruth. Nathan can't wait to see his father every day after work and runs to him. "Poppa! Poppa!"

Mikal swings Nathan up into his arms. "How's my boy?"

Nathan points to David, who has drifted to his mother. "I was playing with him."

Mikal says, "I can see that."

Now David sees them talking about him and comes over.

Nathan repeats, "I was playing with him."

Mikal says, "Nice to meet you, 'him.'"

Not realizing Mikal was joking with him, David corrects him: "I'm not him. I'm David."

Mikal says, "Then nice to meet you, David."

There is instant chemistry, not only between Nathan and David but among Ruth and Rita and Mikal as well. They all leave the park having made friends—the boys as well as the adults.

*

Station Square in the Forest Hills Gardens is where young people congregate after work or a college day. It is through these commons where Hoby and his girlfriend, Norma, and Pat and his girlfriend, Laurie, walk with Daniel and his girlfriend, Edith. Hoby, Pat, and Daniel have each found a partner with whom they have shared the last couple of years. It's hard to discern which of the couples is the most serious. They have all spent a large amount of time together, and their dating has evolved into real relationships. Today is a special celebratory day since this is the evening of the day of the graduation from college for the three young men. It is also a day where all kinds of decisions loom—decisions that they all have put off.

When the friends speak, they are talking to themselves as well as their girlfriends. Hoby's first thought is more a declaration: "Four years? It doesn't seem like that long."

Edith embraces Daniel. Her pride in his accomplishments is obvious. "But my Daniel has four more years of medical school."

Pat and Hoby have finished their education. Hoby says what both he and Pat are thinking. "Daniel wants it that way. And Pat and I have finished our higher education. My folks never thought I'd get into college in the first place."

Pat adds to the sentiment. "It's enough for me too. I don't want to be a doctor."

Hoby chides him, "Besides, no medical school would ever take you and me."

Norma hugs Hoby. "And while Daniel is studying for four years, you and I can find other things to do." She kisses him passionately to demonstrate exactly what she had in mind.

Hoby comes up for air to explain. "See why I love her? She is always on my side." Another kiss between them.

Laurie is less demonstrative, but she feels she has to say something. She says to Pat, "And I want you with me for the next four years too."

Pat is hurt and says, "Just four years?"

Laurie laughs and says, "It's a start."

Edith has listened to the conversation, and the carefree relationship displayed by Norma and Hoby made an impression on her. She watches as Pat and Laurie are now kissing as well. She knows that she and Daniel are not as open as Pat and Laurie and certainly not Hoby and Norma. She attributes his modesty to his childhood in the Ukraine. She takes Daniel's hand. "Come with me."

She leads him away from the others to a secluded part of the gardens. Edith says, "Hoby asked Norma to marry him."

Daniel laughs. "I know. He practiced proposing to Pat and me for about a month."

Edith tests the waters. "And that looks like where Pat and Laurie are heading too."

Daniel didn't want to have this conversation. He tries to stall it. "It's different for me. There's a lot of things I have to do first."

Not what Edith wanted to hear. She probes a bit more. "I can wait—if I know I am what you want."

He kisses her, but even that is more reserved than his two friends with their two girlfriends.

Edith had moved out of her parents' house and into a small flat a few months ago. This was not normal in a Jewish home since young women usually live at home until they marry, but Edith is not a normal young woman. Her mother always refers to her as "my headstrong daughter." For one thing, Edith works as a copy editor for the local newspaper. That is traditionally a man's job, but Edith's skills won her the position. Also, she wanted a place of her own. Part of that reason is Daniel. Daniel lives with Pat and Hoby, and they need a place where they can be alone together.

They enter Edith's small apartment. It is hardly more than a place to return to from work as well as a place to be with Daniel. They kiss in the doorway and shed clothes as they work their way to the bedroom. There, they kiss more passionately before they get onto the bed. Even though they are both nude and about to have sex, she can tell that part of his mind and heart are elsewhere.

She stops him from making love to her. "Don't."

"You want to, don't you?"

She gets out from underneath him and sits up, pulling the covers over her. "Yes, but you don't. Not really."

This takes him by surprise. Their relationship had always involved a lot of sex. "I do."

Edith is bright and intuitive. Yes, their relationship has been a good one, but she has always known there was something else stopping Daniel from completely committing to her. With him graduating and getting ready to pursue a career and a life, she knows that she finally must ask what she has wanted to ask since the first time they were together physically.

"Daniel, there is something else, isn't there?"

He likes Edith. Indeed, she has been there for him. They have shared intimate thoughts and intimate moments. The last thing he wants to do is hurt her.

She realizes she may have been right all along. "I can say I love you. I can say it with all my heart."

Daniel says, "I love you," but he knows it isn't the same as when Edith said it to him, and he knows she is aware of it.

She pulls away to avoid any more intimacy. "But I mean it."

"We've made love before. We've been together for two years."

A line has been crossed. Through tears, Edith tells Daniel, "Don't commit to me because you think you should—or because of the amount of time we've been together. I don't want to be with someone who doesn't feel about me like I feel about him."

Daniel tries to sort out his own feelings. "But you mean more to me than anybody."

It's a stunning realization for Edith, who now knows that their relationship is over. She gets up and puts on her clothes.

"Anybody now. Anybody here. I don't know why it is, but I have had a feeling that this wasn't right. And I think it might be better that we end this now … before we make a mistake. Tell me I'm wrong. Please tell me."

Daniel would, but for a brief moment he remembers being on the hill in Bukachivtski with Rita. He remembers him saying, *"I love you, Rita."*

And he remembers her saying to him, *"I love you, Daniel. No one could love you as much as I do. I always have, and I always will."*

Daniel looks at Edith with compassion and gratitude and then—after a painful moment—answers her honestly. "You're not wrong." She breaks into sobs. He gets up and comforts her since they are close, but both know they are not close enough to continue being together.

CHAPTER TEN

Though Mikal owns New World Lights and Lamps, it never would have thrived if not for Willum Van Hoff. Mikal had bought the store and its inventory, and he thought he could learn the business a little bit at a time. He was proven wrong when one of the first customers who wanted to buy something asked for "a flush mount sconce." Mikal didn't want to admit he didn't know what a flush mount sconce was, so he said, "Why don't you look around and see if there are the exact flush mount sconces that you are looking for?"

Watching the conversation between Mikal and the customer was Willum Van Hoff. After the customer went on his search, Van Hoff came over and said to the customer, "My name is Willum Van Hoff. The sconces are over here. Let me show you."

Who was this Van Hoff? And how did he know more about the store than Mikal, the new owner? When Mikal bought the store, the previous owner had employed Willum Van Hoff. And the old owner hadn't given Van Hoff the courtesy to tell him that the store was being sold. Van Hoff was instantly out of a job, so when Mikal took over, Van Hoff—in hopes that Mikal might need somebody to work at the store—came to see him. Willum was waiting to talk to Mikal when he overheard the customer ask about sconces. That was how the Dutch immigrant came to work alongside Mikal at New World Lights and Lamps and became Mikal's first employee.

*

Medical school is all-consuming for Daniel. Even if he wanted to still have a relationship with Edith, Daniel would hardly have had the time. He barely sees Hoby and Pat. And when they did get together, it was awkward as it would be five of them since Hoby and Pat always brought Norma and Laurie. Hoby and Norma had gotten married. Pat and Daniel were groomsmen, and it wasn't long before Hoby and Norma were expecting a baby.

Time passes. Pat and Laurie have set a date for their wedding. Hoby and Pat tipped off Norma and Laurie that Daniel and Edith were no longer a couple, and Daniel's two friends pleaded with Norma and Laurie that no questions be asked.

Pat put it more strongly. He added to Laurie, more kidding than not: "If you don't want the same thing to happen to you." After the first couple of times when they'd make plans to all go out, Daniel begged off. Even though it was uncomfortable for him, he really did have to focus on medical school. Becoming a doctor had become the entire center of his life.

That said, occasionally he stops by the deli to see Hyman and Rose, who are enormously proud of him. It is as if their own son, Leon, were going on to become a doctor. They tiptoe around the subject of what happened with Edith. Daniel tells them that she just wasn't the one. They understand. Hyman, with a wink to Rose, says to Daniel, "Men know. It took me a long time to finally find Rose."

Rose forgets any disappointment that Daniel and Edith broke up and accepts her husband's statement as a compliment.

At the medical school, Daniel spends his free time with his new friend and classmate Simon. Simon and Daniel have bonded over their love for medicine.

Simon was born with an innate bedside manner, perhaps because Simon's father was a doctor. Simon can't wait to get through med school and obtain his license so he can join his father's private practice.

Daniel's life experience is far different from Simon's, and Simon loves hearing Daniel's stories about the Ukraine and his immigration and what he had to go through to find himself in the same med school class with Simon.

Late one afternoon, Daniel and Simon, still wearing their lab coats, leave a lecture hall and head for the exit of the New York Medical College. It's almost evening, since the classes and lab work run late on a daily basis.

They exit the building, and as they walk off in different directions, Daniel calls to Simon, "See you in the lab tomorrow, friend!"

Simon gives a wave and then circles back to ask, "Daniel, are you doing something tonight?"

With a laugh, Daniel says, "If studying is 'something,' then I'm doing something tonight."

Simon says, "You've got to take your head out of a book once in a while."

Daniel knows Simon is right, but since he broke up with Edith, he really only concentrates on his studies. He calls back, "Thanks. Maybe another time."

With that, Daniel starts down the block. He waits at a corner to let traffic go by, and then he looks up and freezes. It's Rita! He'd know her anywhere!

It probably would only have been a matter of time until he ran into her. He always thought that … always hoped that. And apparently, this was the day. He almost faints from the emotion and steadies himself against a door jamb. He is totally conflicted. He is sure she hasn't seen him since she seemingly is concerned with the young boy by her side. Obviously, it's her son, but Daniel doesn't think about that now. There will be time to think about that, but for now, he can only think: There's Rita. There's Rita! My God, there she is!

Should he call her to her? He could, but should he? Would he be starting something? What if she rejects him? All he can do is stand frozen. She didn't see him, and, breathing hard, he turns and walks away. Maybe it's better this way. But she does live in this neighborhood. That much he assumes.

Rita and Nathan move down the sidewalk. This is the way they always go on their way from the grocery store. Past the park, past the medical school. On this day, something draws her to look down the street. She stops abruptly. She sees Daniel's familiar form. It's been years, but she'd know him anywhere. He's walking away. She could call after him, but she doesn't know what he'd say if she actually talked to him. She is frozen there until Nathan jars her out of her thoughts. "Momma, come on. You said we could get ice cream."

"That's right. I did. Then, let's go, Nathan. Think about what kind you want."

As she walks away with Nathan, she continues to look after Daniel as he disappears down the block. Seeing him, she knows he is still in her heart. And she knows if she has seen him once, she will probably see him again. And what will happen when she does see him again? Not if, but when.

*

Daniel enters his small, undecorated studio apartment. He is still shaken from having seen Rita. He sits on his unmade bed and puts his head in his hands. After a while of contemplating how things could change if Rita were suddenly back in his life, he looks up at the space on his headboard. The same picture from his previous residence that was taken in the Ukraine sits as if it were aware of what has just happened.

*

As is their bedtime tradition, Mikal, still in his business clothes, reads to Nathan. This night it's Mark Twain's *The Prince and the Pauper*. Nathan loves these private times with Mikal. The seven-year-old boy snuggles up against his father. It matters little to him what book Mikal is reading. He just enjoys the sound of his father's voice and the comforting feel of his body next to him.

"Chapter eighteen, 'The Prince with the Tramps.' The troop of vagabonds turned out at early dawn and set forward on their march. There was a lowering sky overhead, sloppy ground underfoot, and a winter chill in the air. All gaiety was gone from the company; some were sullen and silent, some were irritable and petulant, none were gentle-humored, all were thirsty. The Ruffler put 'Jack' in Hugo's charge, with some brief instructions, and commanded John Canty to keep away from him and let him alone; he also warned Hugo not to be too rough with the lad."

Rita never intrudes on these father and son moments. She has Nathan to herself all day long, but today is different.

Even though she won't interrupt, she does have a brief message for her husband: "Mikal, when you're done reading to Nathan, come to bed."

Since Nathan cherishes these moments, he doesn't want his father to rush out and, with pleading eyes, says, "Poppa."

Mikal says to Rita, "When we finish this chapter."

Rita responds, "Okay, but come to me when you can."

She leaves, and Mikal returns to reading. "After a while, the weather grew milder, and the clouds lifted somewhat. The troop ceased to shiver, and their spirits began to improve …" Before long, Nathan falls asleep. Mikal puts in a bookmark, closes the book, kisses Nathan on the forehead, and turns off the light. He moves to the door and closes it. Mikal had sensed an urgency from Rita. Obviously, she has something to tell him about her day. At night in bed is when he usually shares business news from New World Lights and Lamps, and she tells him neighborhood gossip which he calls "News of the Neighborhood."

Mikal enters from reading. Rita is already in bed. As he hangs up his suit jacket in the closet and before he looks back at her, he asks, "So what's the news of the neighborhood?"

"This."

Now he is surprised to see Rita pull down the bed sheet. She is naked and anxious to make love. Mikal is aroused immediately since he has never seen her so stimulated.

All he can say is, "Give me a second."

His coat is already off. His fingers fly to unbutton his shirt; he takes it off, and then strips off his undershirt. He doesn't bother to unlace his shoes, which he kicks off. He unbuttons his pants and lets them fall at his feet and pulls off his underwear as he moves to the bed quickly. If she is this ready, he can be this ready too. He jumps into bed. She kisses him passionately—as if to wipe away the memory of her seeing Daniel. But she can't get Daniel out of her head. Just as Daniel recalls and replays their making love on the hill overlooking Bukachivtski, so does Rita. The vision comes back completely, as if it were happening just a few minutes ago. She remembers opening her arms to Daniel. Though it was in a different language, she remembers him saying, *"I love you, Rita."* And she remembers herself saying, *"I love you, Daniel. No one could love you as much as I do. I always have, and I always will."* And she remembers how much tenderness was in the only time that they made love. She remembers it all. She knows what she promised him, and now, seeing him this afternoon, she wonders what would happen if they did meet.

That memory was years ago. Now, she is in bed with her husband and ready to make love but seeing Daniel in her mind prevents it. And now with Mikal and not with Daniel, she is abruptly no longer eager. The sensitive Mikal recognizes that her mood has changed so suddenly. He pulls away from her. "What is it?"

There is no possible way for her to be honest with her husband. No way for her to explain her feelings. All she can say is, "Just hold me."

He does, tenderly. She clutches him. She is trembling. Though there is no lovemaking, there is a new kind of vulnerability he had not seen in his wife. Their moment is interrupted by a knock at the door. And then the voice of Nathan from the hallway says, "Momma, Poppa, I had a bad dream."

Rita and Mikal look at each other. Any discussion of whatever has changed between them will be delayed as they both reach out to their son. They both race to put on their sleeping garments. Then, Mikal says, "Come on in, then."

Nathan bounds into the room and into their bed. Rita studies his face as he retells his dream: "It was about the prince and the pauper and—"

Nathan stops himself when he looks at his mother. "Momma, you are shaking."

Rita says, "I was worried about your dream."

Mikal looks at his wife and knows there is some other reason. He just doesn't know what it is. Rita knows, and she vows to herself that Mikal will never know.

CHAPTER ELEVEN

The last time Rita saw Daniel, it happened accidentally. Certainly, she could find another way to walk home so that she might not see him, but she doesn't. She can't. She won't. This is where she saw Daniel the previous day. She tells herself that if fate means for her to connect with him, then fate will have its way. She has left Nathan with Ruth to play with David at the park and now walks alone near the medical college. Mixed thoughts play in her head. He did make it to America and is in New York. That much she now knows for certain. And he was coming out of the medical college and wearing a lab coat. That tells her that he has followed his dream to become a doctor. Good for Daniel. She always knew he was smart. And determined. She has always wanted the best for him. She walks slowly and looks where she had seen him, hoping he'd be there. She dallies a bit … hoping against hope. But she doesn't see him. Sadly, she starts away.

Daniel had seen Rita just outside the main building of the medical college. Why was she there? Did she know this was where he was going to medical school? How much did she know about him? How much did he know about her? He knew she married Mikal Gleisserman. He knew she came to America. He saw that she had a child and now knows she lives somewhere near here.

Daniel exits his anatomy classroom with Simon. It is roughly the same time when he had seen Rita. Maybe she'll be there again. But before the classroom door closes behind him and before he can enter the stream of med students, a voice stops him. "Mr. Stabinski, a word."

It's Dr. Gregory. Daniel stops and turns to see his anatomy professor, Dr. Gregory. Simon moves off, a bit jealous that Dr. Gregory had stopped

Daniel and not him. Dr. Gregory is one of the most respected members of the faculty, as well as a high-powered academician who holds a lot of sway at the medical school. The fact that he knows Daniel's name is practically an honor.

Though Daniel wishes to be out on the street to possibly see Rita again, he has no choice but to return to Dr. Gregory. "Yes, Dr. Gregory."

Dr. Gregory says, "I was hoping to talk something over with you."

Dr. Gregory wants to have a word with him? That could be very important for Daniel at the medical college. Still, his heart is pulling him outside. "I was just leaving."

Dr. Gregory is not used to being rejected out of hand. Maybe what he has to say might induce Daniel to speak with him. "It's about the assistant position."

Daniel pauses. He knows that there is every possibility that Rita won't be outside. The assistant position? That is something that every first-year med student would kill for. Dr. Gregory says, "I should think you'd want to talk about it."

Still, Daniel is torn. "I do. I will. Absolutely, but I have to—"

There is something in Daniel's urgent need to leave that strikes a chord in Dr. Gregory, who allows Daniel his freedom to leave by saying, "I guess we could talk about it before class tomorrow."

Daniel is greatly relieved: "Please. Let's. That would be wonderful. If it could please just wait until tomorrow …"

Now Daniel starts to leave again; but knowing the importance of a relationship might be with Dr. Gregory, he crosses back and pumps the professor's hand gratefully before he darts away. Dr. Gregory smiles and returns to his classroom. Daniel rushes out into the street. If he had only been a minute sooner, if only he hadn't paused to shake Dr. Gregory's hand, he might have seen Rita. That briefest of delays keeps them from seeing each other again.

Rita returns from her walk near the medical college and comes upon Ruth watching Nathan and David. At this point, Rita and Ruth's relationship is all about their sons' friendship. Rita watches the boys, who are on swings and matching each other as they go back and forth. Who can go higher?

Rita smiles and says to Ruth, "They play so well together."

Ruth laughs. "I'm glad David met Nathan, or I'd have to be on that swing again."

Rita asks Ruth about Nathan, "How was he?"

"Fine. You have a wonderful son."

"Thank you. It's as if they were meant to be friends."

Ruth comments, "I guess some things are meant to be."

Rita thinks about Daniel and her marriage to Mikal when she responds, "Yes. I guess some things are."

Then Rita looks at her watch. "Well, I have to go." Then, she calls to Nathan, "Time to go, honey!"

Neither Nathan nor David wants to stop swinging. They swing even higher. Ruth and Rita go to the swings and gradually slow down the boys and then stop them. Ruth says, "David, Nathan needs to go now. Maybe Nathan can come over to our place some time."

For David, that possibility eases the pain of Nathan leaving.

Rita confirms, "That would be nice. Maybe we can trade telephone numbers. Will you be here next Tuesday?"

Ruth is as eager as David and tells Rita, "Goodness, we can trade telephone numbers right now."

The boys hear that progress, and both simultaneously yell, "Yay!"

As Ruth looks for a pencil in her large purse, the boys burst into swinging once again.

Rita tells Ruth, "But don't call between six and seven. Mr. Weisborg ties up the party line."

*

Daniel has been hanging around, hoping against hope that she'd be there again. But she isn't. He had no way of knowing that she had been there and hoping to see him as well. Frustrated, he leaves.

Rita takes Nathan by the hand and walks from the park. Nathan says, "Where'd you go, Momma?"

Rita says, "Oh, I had something I had to do."

Nathan says, "Momma, anytime you have something to do, I love to play with David."

More to herself than to Nathan, Rita tells her son, "I'll remember that."

Time passes. Though both Daniel and Rita thought they might run into each other, neither knows each has seen the other. Rita walks by the medical college whenever she can, and Daniel hangs out in front, but the timing has never been right.

*

In the meantime, Daniel had that talk with Dr. Gregory, and he got the position of assistant. When Dr. Gregory says, "Stabinski, I expect to see you here Monday morning at nine."

"I will be here." Daniel is overjoyed. Who can he tell about the good news? He has a drink with Hoby and Pat. Both of them have jobs that they like, and now they are so pleased for Daniel.

Hoby married Norma, and they already have a child on the way. Daniel may not have a serious girlfriend, but according to what he tells them, he is moving ahead in his medical career.

They get drunk to celebrate. This time they are not drinking so Daniel can tell them about a woman, but they are getting drunk out of happiness. Even when he has had three vodkas, Daniel doesn't tell them he saw Rita. God knows what they'd think or what they'd advise him to do.

Then Daniel stops by the deli. Every time he visits, Hyman and Rose get excited. They love hearing him talk about his classes at the medical college, and when he tells them he is now the assistant to one of the top professors, Rose hugs him and cries.

Hyman asks Daniel, "Do you think Dr. Gregory would like some knishes?"

Daniel says, "I'll let you know."

Daniel never shares his feelings about Rita with Hyman and Rose. It's a part of his life he keeps secret—has always kept secret. Besides, there is nothing really to tell anyone about anyway.

Daniel is even more intelligent and capable than Dr. Gregory imagined. Daniel is usually one step ahead of what Dr. Gregory asks of him. It is as if they were colleagues rather than a professor and a student. They work side-by-side on swivel chairs at side-by-side desks.

Today, Dr. Gregory finishes writing a page and closes his lab book. Triumphant, he turns to Daniel. "My hypothesis: With the pituitary gland divided into the two distinct lobes, the anterior lobe growing upward from the pharyngeal tissue at the roof of the mouth and the posterior lobe growing downward from neural tissue varies the functions of the secretions due to the relative positions of its two sources."

Daniel absorbs what Dr. Gregory says, but he thinks about it only briefly before he suggests, "Possibly. But even though you have been working on this long before I joined you, I would say that the pituitary's contiguous structure with the hypothalamus and its attachment by the hypophyseal monitors have a greater effect."

What? Can Daniel actually be so insightful? Dr. Gregory tries to save face: "Which was precisely my conclusion."

They swivel away to have the rest of their conversation face-to-face. Daniel asks, "Were you testing me?"

"No more than your analyses have been testing me."

The two laugh. Dr. Gregory closes his notebook and begins to take off his lab coat. Daniel follows suit. Dr. Gregory says, "That will be all for today. Thank you, Daniel."

Daniel starts to leave. Dr. Gregory stops him with, "And Daniel, thank you for the kasha."

Daniel smiles. "It's knishes."

Dr. Gregory says, "Whatever it is, it's good."

And then Dr. Gregory adds, "Have I told you you're going to make a fine doctor?"

"Many times. And each time, I thank you."

Now Daniel exits into the hallway, which is deserted since Daniel's work with Dr. Gregory keeps him long after the other students have left. He exits the main entrance to leave the building. As always, he looks down the street in hopes of seeing Rita. And to his surprise and amazement, this time he does! He sees her just disappearing around the corner. Daniel doesn't know how to react. He wants to call out to her, but he decides to follow her instead.

Since she hadn't seen Daniel, Rita was discouraged once again. She has no idea that he has caught sight of her and that he is following her down the street. He makes sure that she doesn't see him. He wants to know— needs to know—where she is going, where she lives, what her life is like. He needs to know even before he would think to reveal himself. For many reasons, he is afraid of what might happen if they actually do talk again.

Rita walks toward Mikal's store as Daniel ducks in and out of doorways to avoid being seen.

Inside the successful store, while other customers are browsing and Willum shows a couple some floor lamps, Mikal talks to Mrs. Solomon, an opinionated (but indecisive) woman who has occupied much of his afternoon.

She examines a lamp. "Will this one take a twenty-watt lightbulb?"

Mikal has already answered the same question about every lamp she has looked at. "Mrs. Solomon, it will. Just like the other lamps I already showed you."

She walks around the lamp, examining it from all sides. "I think … yes, I think I like this one."

"Good."

"Could I take it home to try it out? To see how it looks in the living room?"

Willum has ushered the other last customer out the door and now stands by the threshold and waits to close for the day. However, there is still one customer remaining: Mrs. Solomon. Willum gets Mikal's attention and points at his watch. Mikal shrugs to Willum, as if to say, "I'll finish up with this interminable customer. You run along."

Mikal returns to Mrs. Solomon. "Why don't you just buy it and then return it if you don't like it?"

'It's a surprise for my husband."

Anything to get her out of the store. "Then return it if he doesn't like it."

"I would do that, but he doesn't know what he likes. I tell him what he likes."

She suddenly gets indecisive again and inquires, "Could I see the other ones again?"

Hiding his exasperation, Mikal responds, "Which ones?"

"All of them. And can you put them next to each other so I can get a better idea?"

The customer is always right. Biting his tongue, Mikal obliges and says tersely, "All right."

Mikal has disappeared into the storeroom to get the lamps as Rita enters. She is looking for Mikal and crosses to the counter where Mrs.

Solomon waits impatiently. Oddly, it appears as if Mrs. Solomon is the only person in the entire store. Rita crosses to her and greets her, "Hello."

Mrs. Solomon says, "Hello."

Rita says to Mrs. Solomon, "I'm looking for the owner of the store."

Suddenly, Mrs. Solomon gets territorial and indicates the storeroom, "Right now he is helping me."

Rita realizes that Mikal is probably in the back. She settles in. "That's all right. I'll wait."

Mrs. Solomon is just the kind of woman who is judgmental about people—even if she's the one who has caused her to be so. "Between you and me, he takes a long time. See how late it is?"

Rita knows Mikal. He knows how understanding he is with customers, so there is no way Rita would allow anyone to demean him as Mrs. Solomon has done. Rita says defensively, "The store owner is my husband."

Just as Mikal returns, pushing a cart with several lamp candidates for Mrs. Solomon, the demanding woman softens her tone: "Taking your time is a good thing. Having patience is a good quality."

Mikal sees Rita talking to Mrs. Solomon: "Hello, Rita. What are you doing here?"

Rita tells Mikal, "Nathan is at David's, and I thought we could have a dinner for two, but when you didn't come home on time …"

Mikal looks at his customer and tells Rita, "I was helping Mrs. Solomon."

This puts Mrs. Solomon's back up. She concludes and spits out, "I know when I've been insulted."

Mrs. Solomon probably gets "insulted" that way often. She turns and exits the store. When she huffily gets outside and moves down the street, she passes Daniel, who has followed Rita to the store.

So, this is where Rita has gone! He edges up to the store window and is still careful not to be seen. He looks inside and sees Rita talking to Mikal. He sees them, but he can't hear them.

Rita is saying to Mikal, "Did I ruin the sale for you?"

Mikal responds, "No, and I thank you. You hurried her up. She wasn't going to buy anything anyway."

"How can you tell?"

Mikal smiles and says, "The longer people look, the less chance they will buy."

Rita is impressed with her husband's understanding of people. "That's Talmudic reasoning."

Mikal laughs and jokes, "What can I say? I'm Jewish." Then he adds, "You have a wise husband—a wise, hungry husband."

Rita says, "Then let's go."

As Mikal goes to the storeroom to get his coat, Rita looks at one of the lamps Mrs. Solomon failed to buy.

Outside the store, Daniel peers in to see Rita, to get a better look at her in the light. But as she starts to look toward the street, he ducks away, not wishing to be seen by her—not this way, anyway. His heart beats with the emotion that he is this close to her.

Mikal returns with his coat, and they walk to the front door.

Daniel is nowhere to be seen as Mikal locks up.

*

On another day, a rainy day, Rita walks by the medical college, hoping to see Daniel. She always hopes to see Daniel. She doesn't. Hopefully, another day. Because she saw him in the lab coat, she has made the accurate assumption that he attends this school. But today, Daniel isn't there.

New World Lights and lamps is doing better and better. Mikal and Willum are both tied up with customers when Daniel enters. Daniel has taken off his lunch hour, and instead of eating, he has come into Mikal's store. He assumes Rita won't be there. Besides, Daniel is not there to see Rita. He feigns looking at a lamp when Willum finishes with a customer and approaches Daniel. "May I help you?"

Daniel tells him, "Yes, you can. I've got a new place to live, and I was hoping to have someone help me pick out a lamp."

Willum hears Daniel's accent and recognizes that Mikal has a fellow countryman in the store. Making sure, Willum asks Daniel, "Are you Russian?"

Daniel says, "I am from Ukraine."

Willum replies, "I'm from Holland, but the owner of the store, Mikal Glass, is from the Ukraine."

Daniel smiles at the "coincidence."

Willum calls off to Mikal, "Mr. Glass!"

Mikal looks up to see Willum speaking with Daniel. The man he is talking to holds a lamp when Willum continues, "This man is from the Ukraine."

Mikal tells his customer, "If you would take the lamp to the sales desk, I will be there in a minute."

The man carries the lamp to the counter as Mikal crosses to Willum and Daniel. Daniel measures Mikal. Mikal is the man who took his Rita away. Of course, Daniel bears animosity, but he hides those feelings. Daniel has come this far. What now?

CHAPTER TWELVE

In Mikal and Rita's home, Rita prepares dinner in the kitchen while Nathan plays with blocks, where he makes a fortress. He sits in the middle, pretending he can't get out. He calls urgently to his mother in the other room, "Is Poppa coming home soon?"

Rita stirs some soup and calls back, "Always the same time; always the same question."

Rita leaves the simmering pot to duck her head into the living room. "Why is it so important?"

Nathan has quite an imagination. Though the "fort" is only three inches tall, he says, "Poppa has to get me out of this fort. I'm stuck in here."

Rita laughs. "That's a problem, all right."

Nathan says, "And he promised to listen to me read."

"Then he will. Your poppa always keeps his promises."

She turns back to getting dinner ready when the front door opens, and Nathan, knowing it will be Mikal, leaps out of the fort and knocks over the rest of the blocks as he goes to the door when Mikal enters.

"Poppa!"

Mikal swoops Nathan into his arms and says, "I'm home and such a greeting."

Rita gives a last stir of the soup and goes to the door as well. They give a greeting kiss. Nathan breaks them up to get attention. "Poppa! Look at my fort!"

Mikal looks over at what is now a pile of blocks. "Very nice."

And Nathan keeps going. "Poppa, you have to listen to me read. Momma and I went to the library, and we brought home a Hans Christian Andersen story."

Mikal jokes, "What would be wrong with a Hans Jewish Andersen story?"

Nathan is confused. "Is there a Hans Jewish Andersen?"

Rita elbows Mikal. "Nathan, your poppa is making a joke."

Now Mikal has an announcement. "Nathan, you brought home a story, and I brought home a surprise."

Nathan is bursting. "Is it a new bicycle?"

Mikal says, "No. It's a surprise for the whole family. Someone from the old country. I brought someone home for dinner."

Rita wishes she had told him. She hasn't prepared enough dinner. "Why didn't you call?"

"I tried, but Weisborg was on the line. He's always on the line. We have to talk to Weisberg about that. Besides, this way, it's more of a surprise."

Mikal ducks out of the door and ushers in Daniel, who had made Mikal stop along the way so he could buy a bottle of wine. Rita sees Daniel and is dumbstruck. She looks at Daniel. He looks at her. Can this really be happening? They both know what they promised each other so long ago; but time has passed, yet immediately all those old feelings are here. They instantly realize that they must mask any emotions they have—though that is practically impossible.

Apparently, Mikal sees none of it. He is proud that he brought home someone from their old country. Mikal says, "You must know him. He said he thinks he knew you in Bukachivtski."

The omnipresent Nathan pipes into the conversation, "I don't know him."

Mikal tousles the boy's hair: "That's because you were born in America."

Nathan says, "I guess that's it."

Daniel stares into Rita's eyes. "Oh, yes. Rita Rabinovich. It is you. I remember."

Then Daniel turns to Rita, "Do you remember?"

Still hiding their relationship from Mikal, she stares into Daniel's eyes. "I remember too."

Mikal still doesn't grasp the latent intensity between Rita and Daniel. Why would he? Mikal is merely proud that he brought their fellow countryman to their house. He says to Daniel, "Then you did know my wife?"

Difficult as it may be, Daniel takes his gaze from Rita and says to Mikal, "Yes, I did. A little. But that was long ago."

Rita gasps. Does the gasp let out their secret?

Mikal says, "What's the matter?"

She covers. "I ... I just never heard this man speak English before."

Daniel says to Rita, "And I never heard you either."

As if to defuse the moment, Rita says, "Yes, some things change. But I am not Rita Rabinovich anymore. I am Rita Glass now."

Mikal explains, "It was Gleisserman. They changed our name when we came to America. You know they like things simple in this country."

Daniel says firmly, "I am still Daniel Stabinski. I wouldn't let them change me. I still feel the same way I always have."

Mikal says to Rita, "Daniel is a doctor."

Daniel corrects him, "Almost a doctor. I have one more year of study left."

Rita says, "I think I remember that you said you wanted to be a doctor."

Their conversation was and is rife with double meanings. Daniel says pointedly, "It was part of my dream. Sometimes a dream works out."

Mikal wants Daniel to feel more at home. "Let me take your coat, Daniel. Make yourself comfortable."

Mikal takes the coat from Daniel and hangs it in the closet while putting his arms around Rita and explaining, "I was unfair to my Rita. She didn't have time to make more food for another person."

Daniel settles into a chair. "Anything is fine. I am not married, and whatever you have is better than what I usually have."

This is information that Rita wanted to know. Daniel is not married. She admires the way that Daniel has let her know that.

Rita announces, "We can divide up the meat, and I can add a few potatoes."

"Anything is fine."

Rita escapes Mikal's arms and returns to the kitchen—not just to cook but to catch her breath.

Nathan wants to be around Mikal and their guest.

Mikal wants to talk to Daniel about his journey. Mikal says to Nathan, "Help your mother."

Nathan knows what that means and scurries into the kitchen. Mikal and Daniel talk.

Mikal says to Daniel, "You were right. You said you knew her. Tell me: Is she the same person?"

Daniel does his best to disguise the awkwardness of the situation. "Yes, it's the Rita I remember, but all of us change some."

Mikal is so pleased that he brought Daniel home. "Isn't this something? We all lived so far away and so long ago, and now we're here together."

Daniel tries to deflect talking about any relationship that he and Rita have had and changes the subject: "Mikal, your big store—you have done well for yourself."

"I had an advantage. I started with something. You ... you became a doctor. And the way you tell it: from nothing."

"Almost a doctor."

"Right. Almost a doctor."

In the kitchen, with Nathan hanging on her dress, Rita tries to hide her emotional tears while she cooks at the stove. The perceptive little boy sees this. "Potatoes make you cry too, Momma? You said it was onions."

"These are special kinds of potatoes."

The dinner is eventful. Not because of what is said but because of what isn't. When Rita passes the potatoes to Daniel, there is a pause. When Daniel opens the wine and pours some in Rita's glass, there is a moment. These stolen glances seemingly remain unnoticed by Mikal, but they are ever so meaningful to Rita and Daniel.

During the meal, Nathan has been chattering away about his friend David and the games they play in the park. Daniel studies Rita's son. He has her hair color, as he should, but there is something more familiar about him.

Mikal says to Nathan, "Help clean the table like always."

Nathan says to Daniel, "If it's like always, we eat in the kitchen."

A bit of an embarrassment to both Rita and Mikal. Mikal says to Nathan, "Just go."

As Nathan starts to clear dishes, Mikal explains, "Nathan means that we only eat in this room on special occasions."

Daniel responds, "Then you think I am a special occasion?"

Rita answers very quickly, "Yes." But then she covers equally quickly. "Mikal has a lot of family. When they come over, we always eat around this table."

Rita hands a finished plate to Nathan, who has just returned from the kitchen. He takes this one and as many other plates as his small hands can muster before he takes them into the kitchen.

Daniel watches him go. "You have a nice son."

Rita speaks for both herself and Mikal when she says, "He's a joy."

Then Mikal stands. "Come, let us go into the other room where we can be more comfortable."

Mikal takes off his shoes and puts on his slippers. He says to Daniel, "You can take off your shoes too."

Daniel says, "I will, but I have to warn you."

Daniel takes off his shoes, and there is a hole in one of his socks. He wiggles his toe through it. Almost as old friends, the three of them laugh.

Mikal says, "If you had a wife, she would never let you leave the house unless she darned the sock. Rita wouldn't." Then he turns to Rita. "Right?"

Rita says, "Right."

Mikal says to Daniel, "I'm surprised that a man who is almost a doctor didn't find someone to marry."

Rita and Daniel look at each other. Mikal is unaware that he is talking in a sensitive area. Daniel answers, "Being a medical student takes up a lot of time."

Mikal opines, "Doctors get married."

Daniel looks squarely at Rita and responds, "I suppose I didn't find the right woman yet."

Mikal goes on. "It was easier in the old country, the old ways. My papa found Rita for me. Maybe we can find someone for you."

He turns to Rita. "What do you think about my sister Hannah? Do you think she'd like to marry a doctor?"

Rita says, "Is that why you invited Daniel here? To marry off your fat sister?"

Mikal has another idea. "What about my clerk Willum's sister, Fanny?"

Rita objects to this idea too. "The cross-eyed one? You are such a yenta."

Having finished putting the dishes in the sink, Nathan enters from the kitchen and talks to Mikal. "All the dishes are away. Poppa, now can you hear me read?"

Mikal is torn. He'd rather stay and visit longer with Daniel. Rita answers for him. "You go, Mikal. Daniel and I have some catching up to do."

Mikal grumbles and then kids as he uses his hands to demonstrate how fat Hannah is. "Is it because I mentioned fat Hannah, and (he crosses his eyes)?"

They laugh, as does Daniel. Nathan tugs at Mikal. "Come, Poppa. I want to finish the book before I fall asleep reading."

That seals the deal, and Mikal rises to go off with Nathan. He turns to Daniel. "Goodnight, Daniel. It's so nice to make a new old friend."

Daniel and Rita wait to speak until Mikal is out of the room. "Daniel says to her, "He's a nice man."

Rita says, "I know. I was lucky."

Daniel says, "And I really like your son."

"Thank you."

They pause to collect their thoughts—probably both thinking the same thing, since Daniel asks, "How old is Nathan?"

Rita answers quickly, as if that changes things. "Seven years and one month."

Daniel has already done the calculations, and he says what Rita already suspects. "He could be … and I see it in his eyes."

Rita looks off to the bedroom where Mikal and Nathan have gone. She says, "We cannot talk about this now."

Daniel moves very close to her. "Then when?"

Rita never thought she would see Daniel again. And she never thought she'd ever have to cope with what they both assume to be true. She tries to move away from him. "Daniel, even if—"

Daniel won't let the matter drop. "When can we talk? Really talk."

"I don't know if we ever can."

He persists, "We have to talk."

Rita knows there is no escaping it, even if she wanted to. She gives in. "The East River overlook at Third Street. Tomorrow at two. Can you get away?"

Daniel says firmly, "I will get away."

In the bedroom, Nathan haltingly reads to Mikal. "'Poor little ugly duckling!' the mother duck would say. 'Why are you so different from the others?' And the ugly duckling felt worse than ever. He secretly wept at night. He felt nobody wanted him. 'Nobody loves me, they all tease me! Why am I different from my brothers?'"

CHAPTER THIRTEEN

Dr. Gregory is going over a new theory as the upbeat Daniel is on his way past the lab. Though the two of them have been working side-by-side, they never discuss anything personal. It's not that they wouldn't. They just don't. Dr. Gregory is pleased that Daniel works with him and can't wait to show him some new findings. "Daniel, I'm glad you're here. Come look at this."

Daniel slows down. He really hadn't planned to stop by the lab. Still, Dr. Gregory is his boss, so Daniel reluctantly enters. There is someplace else he must be.

Dr. Gregory neither notices Daniel's reticence, nor does he care where else Daniel has to be. He tells Daniel, "I dyed the cells on the tissue sample, and I was right. There was no significant growth in the—" Dr. Gregory stops himself.

He sees that Daniel isn't wearing his lab coat. "I'm sorry. No lab coat. I must assume you didn't come in to listen to this. What is it?"

Daniel confesses, "I just want to know if I can leave early today."

Daniel never asks for personal favors. Dr. Gregory obliges, but he can't resist teasing Daniel. "Something more important than membrane mutations? I can't believe that."

Daniel appreciates Dr. Gregory letting him go and admits more honestly than not. "Yes. This one time."

"Okay, then. See you tomorrow."

"Thank you."

Daniel leaves—and quickly, before the professor changes his mind.

It's a gray day at the Third Street overlook. Rita has deliberately chosen this lightly traveled area. Daniel wears a topcoat as he approaches and stops when he sees Rita, who has been waiting and pondering exactly how to talk to Daniel about what they need to talk about. Rita is bundled in a coat and warm scarf as well. Although he sees her in front of him, his mind recalls a sunny day a long time ago when the young Daniel and she were untroubled, and all they cared about was each other. In his memory, she is smiling at him, loving him. Then, suddenly it is today, and this Rita turns and smiles at him with that same smile. Silently, he moves next to her in the same way he was remembering. The palpable heat between them remains electric. They come together but make no effort to touch.

Daniel asks quietly, "Are you happy?"

That question can be interpreted in so many ways. Rita answers just as quietly. "Happy that we've found each other again? Yes."

Daniel nods. He is pleased that Rita brought the question back to the two of them. He asks, "I mean, are you happy in your life?"

She deflects. In a way, she doesn't want to confront her own mixed emotions. "Mikal is a good man."

Daniel dignifies the response. "You could only be with a good man."

"Thank you for that."

"And Nathan is a great boy."

"I know that."

Now the subject that both had been trying to avoid, the subject that has been living in Daniel's mind since he considered the possibility. He looks squarely at Rita and says, "And he could be my great boy."

If that were true, so much would unravel. She doesn't know what she wants. For now, all she chooses to say is, "That is something we don't know for sure."

They don't speak for a while. Then, in the gentlest of ways, he reaches out to take her hand. She clasps his. The electricity is there—still there. Whatever has transpired, she still feels the same way. Daniel must know more. "I asked if you were happy."

Not dropping his hand, Rita has to acknowledge the truth. "As happy as I would have been with you? I can't answer that. I don't know how to answer that."

Daniel stares deeply into her eyes, the eyes he had stared deeply into back in the Ukraine. The eyes that have been part of his soul for as long as he can remember. He whispers, "I can." He moves to kiss her. She resists. He persists. There is a moment … a moment Daniel believes seeing her again was something that she couldn't cope with. He doesn't know what to do next. Any decision is taken from him when Rita gives in to her emotions, and she reaches for him and kisses him—a long and tender kiss—a kiss filled with their past and now with their present, though neither can predict what their future might be.

Then Rita lets her mind rule her heart. She backs away from him. "We must not."

Daniel won't let his dreams be crushed so easily, not when he sees that a part of Rita wants what he wants. "Why not? Because many years ago, your father took happiness away from us?"

The thought is not lost on Rita. She tells Daniel something he could not know. "My father died."

Daniel says, "I'm sorry about that, but now you don't owe your father anything. You paid him enough already."

Part of her won't allow her to break her vow. "I'm married."

"Don't you think that I know that? But we—you and me—we were the ones who were supposed to be married."

Rita's heart and mind are fighting. "Daniel, we can't. You have a life that's good. You're going to be a doctor."

"My life will never be good unless you are in it. You said, 'I will always love you. No one could love you as much as I do. I always have, and I always will.' That's what you said."

"I know what I said."

She kisses him again to let him know that she meant it then, and she means it now. Still, she is torn. Giving in to Daniel now will throw her life upside down. It will affect not just the two of them but Mikal and Nathan. Rita is a good person. She doesn't want to hurt anybody. "There are other people."

Daniel knows who she means, but he won't walk away from her. "Kiss me again."

This time, she won't. "We cannot do this."

"Because you don't love me anymore?"

The truth is too overwhelming for her. "No. Because I do."

Daniel stares at her. She stares back. They melt into each other and kiss. He takes her hand and leads her away.

They enter Daniel's med school apartment. She stands at the door as if she were about to comment on the furnishings, the decor. For a moment he makes light of his place. "It's not Bukachivtski, but it's home."

But Daniel is not interested in her opinion as to how he is living as a single man. Instead, he immediately brings her into his bedroom. He had hoped this is how the day would be—that he would bring Rita back here. He wished, anyway. He had laid a sunflower on the bed. She sees the sunflower, appreciates all that sunflowers mean to them, and then her eye is caught by the picture of herself and Daniel on the nightstand.

She stares at him. "You keep this here?"

"Always." But then Daniel sees no reason not to be honest with her. "Unless I was bringing someone back."

"There were other women?"

"Yes."

"Lots of other women?"

Daniel doesn't see why he should be questioned about his loyalty. He just says, "What can I say?"

She realizes that none of his history without her should matter. Instead, she grabs him and kisses him more passionately than she ever has. Not even breaking from their kiss, clothes come off sensually, and the two once lovers and about to be lovers again gracefully find their way to the bed. While they are there naked, they admire each other's bodies. Daniel says, "You are more beautiful than ever, and now more real than I ever could have dreamed."

As if to prove to each other how real this is, they slowly kiss every inch of each other. Every inch is proof of their lasting love. Only then, do they actually make love. Passionate, aggressive, wanton sex that they unleash as if they can't help themselves, and they can't. Then when he is inside her again, he stops. Before he climaxes, he fixes his gaze on the woman he has always loved. She returns his look, and they push each other to even more powerful orgasms, sensations that grip their bodies, hearts, and souls. What will their future be? Neither thinks about that now. All they can think about is being lost in each other.

CHAPTER FOURTEEN

Carrying a large folder, Mikal enters the lobby of the New York hospital. It's a new world for him. Other than when he was at a hospital to see Nathan come into the world, he had not been in a hospital. Nurses and doctors move back and forth across the lobby with warranted importance. He feels that he would be impeding medical practice to slow one down to even ask a question, but after waiting several minutes, he sees a nurse who is about to leave the hospital at the end of her shift. He stops her. "May I ask a question?"

The nurse sees that something is troubling him. "How can I help you?"

"I'm looking for a doctor."

She grows immediately more professional. "What's the matter?"

"Nothing. It's more a personal matter. I'm looking for Dr. Daniel Stabinski."

"Dr. Stabinski? Oh, yes. He's finishing rounds before he goes back to the lab. All graduate school med students need to make rounds."

"Where would I find him?

She points to a ward off the lobby. "That way."

She leaves. Mikal sighs and then looks at the door where the nurse pointed.

He knows that by going through that door and facing Daniel, lives will change. But it has to be done. He edges to the swinging door and passes through, hoping to see Daniel down the hallway, but no doctors are visible.

Inside an elderly patient's room, Daniel examines a healing incision while he speaks softly to the woman, a woman eager to leave the hospital.

"Mrs. Goldblum, you're healing nicely. You should be able to go home in two days."

The disappointed woman says, "Two days? The holidays are coming. I have to go now. Who is going to make my brisket?"

Daniel says gently, "I know you want to leave—that your family needs you—but you don't want to go home and come back worse because you left too early, do you?"

He has gotten through to her. "All right. You probably know what you're talking about."

He says, "I try."

He leaves her room and moves into the hallway, where he looks up and sees Mikal. Mikal? Here? Why? Could Mikal know about him and Rita? Rita would never tell him. Why is he here? The best thing for Daniel to do is to greet Mikal and to pretend that nothing has happened between him and Rita.

Mikal hasn't determined exactly what to say to Daniel when they come together. Daniel speaks first. "Mikal, good to see you. Are you feeling all right?"

The moment of truth for Mikal. "I'm feeling fine." Then he holds up the large folder. "Would you look at this chart?" As Mikal looks on, Daniel opens the folder and pulls out a binder. In the binder is a medical chart with Mikal's name on it. Even with a cursory glance, Daniel appreciates its significance.

Daniel looks around and sees an empty patient's room. "Come with me."

Daniel leads Mikal into the room. Mikal says to Daniel, "Dr. Jacoby gave me a copy of the results of the test. See what it says?"

Daniel confirms, "Yes. It says you can never have children."

"Never. I went to see Dr. Jacoby to see if Rita and I could have another one after Nathan, but the doctor says we can't. I thought Nathan must have been a miracle. That's what I thought. Then the doctor said that I never could have produced children. I didn't know what to think. Rita never knew that I went to the doctor for the tests."

Mikal looks Daniel right in the eye. Daniel doesn't look away. At this point, there is no use in denying what Mikal is about to say. Mikal is angry, and Daniel can't blame him.

"Nathan is not my son. You're the real father of my Nathan. Tell me that isn't true."

Daniel doesn't refute it. "It's true."

Daniel lets Mikal vent. "You and my Rita. Back in the Ukraine. I thought I saw something between you when you came over. Do you deny that you were in love with her?"

Daniel feels for Mikal, but he won't back away from how he feels about Rita. "No."

Mikal goes on. "And I counted the months before he was born. I am a businessman. I know arithmetic. They said that Nathan came early. I believed that. Why wouldn't I believe it?"

The two are at a loss. What to do now? Neither knows.

Mikal says, "How am I supposed to live with this?"

Daniel says, "And how am I?"

They stand looking at each other. Neither knows exactly what to do next.

Daniel says, "Are we going to fight?"

Mikal isn't the fighting type. And Daniel abhors violence. Finally, Mikal tries to garner sympathy from Daniel. "I have always loved her.'

Daniel says, "So have I." Saying that he was in love with her before she even knew Mikal would serve no purpose.

Mikal takes back the chart and says, "What can either of us do about it now?"

Daniel, who usually has answers, this time has none. "I don't know."

Daniel starts to move away from Mikal, but Mikal blocks his path. "You have ruined my life. How can I go home to my son and wife?"

Daniel is also torn as to how to proceed. He could say, "Go home to your wife and my son." But he doesn't. What purpose would that serve?

Devastated, but trying to find the strength, Mikal turns and leaves the room. He walks out into the hallway. Daniel follows him and watches Mikal go through the swinging door leading to the lobby. Obviously, Mikal doesn't know that Daniel and Rita have been together and have an ongoing relationship.

*

Daniel and Rita are together again in Daniel's apartment. They are in his bedroom where they spend all their time when they are here. They are entwined, having just finished making love. He is lost in thought and pulls away from her. She knows him well enough to know that he is troubled. "What? What is it?"

Daniel knows he must tell her about Mikal's visit to the hospital. There is no way to soften the news. "Mikal came to the hospital."

Rita is alarmed. "Oh, my God. Oh, my God. What does he know? How much does he know?"

"He showed me some tests. He can't have children. He could never have had children."

"Then he knows that Nathan isn't his son?"

"And he said he could tell I was with you when he saw the looks between us when I came to dinner. He put it together."

"Mikal is a smart man."

Without saying anything else, Rita gets up and starts to put on her clothes. Daniel stops her momentarily. "He doesn't know anything about us being together like this now."

"Who knows what Mikal knows? I have to go. I can't do this. Not anymore."

Daniel dreads that he is losing her again. "But—"

Rita pushes past him. "I will always love you."

He can't stop her. He knows it. "But I just found you after having lost you."

As Rita leaves him, she says woefully, "Please. Please don't find me again."

CHAPTER FIFTEEN

Whatever is happening with Mikal and Rita and Daniel, the day-to-day work at New World Lights and Lamps goes on—with more and more success. Mikal hires a new employee, the awkward but anxious-to-please Jerome. Jerome was born without a right hand, but he has adapted and can do just about anything using his left hand. The goodhearted Mikal hired him despite Jerome's disability. Jerome is still learning the lighting business, and Willum keeps an eye on him.

While Jerome shows different lights and lamps to other customers, Willum is tied up showing a lamp to an elderly Jewish man, Mr. Lefkowitz, who asks yet another question, "Do you have to dust it?"

Willum answers honestly, "All our lamps need dusting."

Mr. Lefkowitz doesn't like the honest answer, so he asks, "Is there a store that sells lamps that don't need dusting?"

The quick-thinking Willum comes up with another way to make a sale. "Mr. Lefkowitz, what you want is a light that comes from the ceiling. That way, nobody is tall enough to see the dust."

The elderly Jewish man inquires, "Do you have any like that?"

Willum replies, "Just your luck. It just so happens we have a large collection of them."

Then Willum calls off, "Jerome! Could you show Mr. Lefkowitz the chandeliers?"

Jerome hears his name as well as the request. "Right away."

Mikal is not in the store. For the last few days, Mikal has taken time from his day to go walking alone. The news of Nathan's true father causes him anguish that he takes inside. He walks down the block, past the fish market, along the seaside where he usually stops to look out at the Statue of Liberty, as if to say to himself, "Is this what happens when you come to America?"

Mikal thinks that Rita is unaware that Nathan is Daniel's child, but for the boy's sake, he can't let her know that. This obviously troubles him, but keeping this secret is what Mikal feels he must do.

At the same time, Mikal is unaware of the ongoing affair between Rita and Daniel, which is the secret that Rita had kept from her husband. Secrets among the three abound. Rita's intense, passionate love for Daniel and their history was too important for her to have given up Daniel.

At New World Lights and Lamps, Mikal and Willum have become true friends. Willum thinks it strange that his boss/friend leaves the store in the middle of the day for no apparent reason, but it is Mikal's store, and he can do whatever he wants. Mikal has never shared with Willum the reason for his distraction. Mikal has never shared the reason with anyone, not even his family members. And he has not shared with Rita the fact that he and Daniel met, and he has not shared the knowledge that Nathan is not his son. It's as if not talking about it might somehow change the truth.

Willum sees Mikal's return and goes to him. Willum is proud of the number of customers in the store. Mikal sees how much activity is going on. Willum tells Mikal, "Business is booming."

"Business is booming" is what Mikal and Willum say to each other when there is even more than one customer in the store. It is their little joke with each other.

Mikal thinks to himself: "At least Willum is loyal to me."

With that thought, he pulls Willum aside. "How long have you been working here, Willum?"

Willum knows exactly how long. "Five months and two weeks."

Mikal says, "I think it's time you became a manager."

Willum is floored. This is something that they had never even discussed. "Really?"

The two men shake hands, and Mikal confirms, "Yes, really. You have earned it." Mikal lays out what that means. "You know you won't get commissions anymore." Mikal goes on. "But what you lose in sales, you more than make up when I double your salary."

Willum is so grateful that all he can do is repeat his surprise: "Really?" and shakes Mikal's hand even more rigorously.

While the men are engaged, Rita enters. She is still bundled up and still shaken from her tryst with Daniel and the new knowledge that Daniel and Mikal have met. She passes through the customers and clerks and comes over to Mikal, who hides what he knows about Nathan from her. Mikal says to his wife, "Rita, meet our new store manager, Willum."

Until recently, Mikal and Rita had discussed any changes at the store with each other, but not anymore. The store is now a refuge where Mikal can be honest with himself.

Willum is so excited about his promotion he tells Rita, "Your husband just told me. I am so happy."

Rita is truly pleased for Willum. "That's very nice for you. I am happy for you as well."

Willum senses the unexpected coolness between Mikal and Rita, who had always seemed like the happiest of couples. He knows enough not to ask. He goes off to tell Jerome his good news. "Jerome, guess who you're talking to. Me. The new store manager!"

Jerome shakes Willum's hand.

On the other side of the store amid the floor lamp fixtures, Mikal turns to Rita. "Where is Nathan?"

"He's fine. He's at Ruth's." An icy statement of the necessary information. That is enough for Mikal and Rita for now. They both do what they feel is right for Nathan.

CHAPTER SIXTEEN

During the three years after the confrontation between Daniel and Mikal, Daniel and Rita try to stop seeing each other, but the attraction is too great. They need each other. Both are careful not to be discovered. Is it possible to love two men? Rita doesn't think about it. She won't think about it. She just follows her heart.

Daniel graduates from the medical college at the top of his class and becomes a physician. He talks with Dr. Gregory. During their work together, Dr. Gregory always knew that Daniel wanted to be a physician and to treat patients, but he was happy enough to have had Daniel for the time he did. Conversely, Daniel's friend Simon always wanted to work in a lab prior to joining his father in his medical practice. Daniel recommends Simon to Dr. Gregory. Simon is no Daniel, but he is dedicated, and that is important to Dr. Gregory, who accepts Simon as his new colleague.

Daniel has a second-floor office at the hospital, which is attached to the medical college. He makes it a point to be in his office on Tuesdays at 3:30 because at that time, Rita walks by with Nathan.

Rita looks up at the window and knows that Daniel is there. When he sees her, he gives a small wave. That's how they've arranged it. Though Daniel can't be in Nathan's life, he can see how his son is growing.

It's raining on this particular Tuesday, and Rita and Nathan both carry umbrellas. Rita is sure that Daniel is looking down as he always does, so she tilts Nathan's umbrella away from his face so that Daniel can get a better view of the boy.

Nathan says, "It's pouring rain, Mom. Can't we go the short way? Why do we always have to go the long way?"

Rita has no explanation except to say, "No, Nathan. I like to go this way."

Nathan decides to get back at his mother. "Okay for you." With that, he splashes wildly in a puddle to show his displeasure. Rita laughs at her son's antics. She glances up at Daniel's window. Daniel has witnessed the boy's behavior and admires the boy's independence. He smiles before he leaves his office to return to his patients.

*

While Daniel works diligently at the hospital and Mikal's store continues to do well, Daniel and Rita find time to be together. Nathan is growing, but the world is turning upside down. Beginning with the assassination of Archduke Ferdinand in Sarajevo, the nations of the world are hurtling toward a global war.

Rita, Daniel, and Mikal had fled the upheaval in Europe, but the new overseas strife will soon engulf them as well as all of America. At first, most Americans feel that the war is Europe's problem. They hope so, anyway, but merchant ships are sunk. President Wilson wins his second election with the campaign slogan "He kept us out of war," but the entrance into the fighting is quickly becoming inevitable. The sinking of the *Lusitania* and the loss of more than a thousand American lives is the death knell for America's isolationism.

At the end of his address to Congress, President Wilson declares:

> "It is a distressing and oppressive duty, Gentlemen of the Congress, which I have performed in thus addressing you. There are, it may be, many months of fiery trial and sacrifice ahead of us. It is a fearful thing to lead this great peaceful people into war, into the most terrible and disastrous of all wars, civilization itself seeming to be in the balance. But the right is more precious than peace, and we shall fight for the things which we have always carried nearest our hearts—for democracy, for the right of those who submit to authority to have a voice in their own Governments, for the fights and liberties of small nations, for a universal dominion of right by such a concert of free

people as shall bring peace and safety to all nations and make the world itself at last free. To such a task, we can dedicate our lives and our fortunes, everything that we are and everything that we have, with the pride of those who know that the day has come when America is privileged to spend her blood and her might for the principles that gave her birth and happiness and the peace which she has treasured. God helping her, she can do no other-"

*

Most of the time when Mikal's family comes to Shabbat dinner on Friday evening, the discussion is about work or the kids or planning next week's Shabbat dinner, but this time, it is decidedly different. Even the prayer over the candles has an added significance. The prayer has always been for shalom—for peace. And now its significance is more meaningful than they ever could have imagined.

Mikal and Rita look around the table at the assembled. As food is passed around, their eyes fix on Josef and Sid. Both men are of the age that they will be called to join the army. Mikal is older, so he won't have to serve, but both of his brothers will probably have to enter the armed forces and go back across the sea to fight in lands they had chosen to leave.

Mikal is not a talker; he especially doesn't like to speak in public or even at Shabbat dinners, but tonight he feels compelled to say something.

"I am happy we are all together at a time like this. We all came to this country for its freedom, and our president has said that we have to fight to save that freedom. My two brothers, you may have to serve. They say I am too old, but you should know I would. And if you are called, I am here for the family, because that is what is important—family."

Mikal is emotional. Rita likes that about him and kisses his cheek as each of his brothers' wives kiss their husbands. The future is unknown for all of them. The subject hangs over the table in the flickering light from the candles.

*

Daniel comes down the block and passes a line of young men waiting to enlist at the army recruiting station. The seriousness of the war is not lost on Daniel, and he has made a decision. He continues on to Greenbaum's Deli. He hasn't been there for a while, but it looks the same. It always looks the same. He looks in the window and sees Hyman behind the counter. Hyman looks a little older, but just seeing him brings a smile to Daniel's face. It feels like home. He enters and waits as Hyman finishes taking an order from Mrs. Gross, a new customer.

Mrs. Gross says to Hyman, "Mrs. Epstein says that your corned beef is the best in the city."

Hyman answers, "Mrs. Epstein knows what she's talking about."

"But she said to make sure to get the leanest," adds Mrs. Gross.

He points to the corned beef marked leanest. He takes it out and puts it on the scale. "How much do you want?"

"A pound."

Daniel appreciates that Hyman is still up to his old tricks. As Hyman starts laying out the slices of corned beef, he looks up and sees Daniel. Daniel coming back is always big news around the deli. Excited, he calls off, "Rose, Daniel's here!"

Almost trotting, Rose appears from the back. She comes right up to Daniel and hugs him. As soon as Mrs. Gross takes the corned beef, pays, and leaves the deli, Hyman joins Daniel and Rose. Hyman grabs the closed sign and puts it in the window so they can put their full attention on Daniel. Hyman says, "You're going to tell us everything."

Rose can't agree more. "Everything, Daniel."

Daniel says, "That's why I'm here."

As they sit in a booth, Daniel so enjoys their warmth. Rose grabs some pickles for Daniel to nosh on while they talk. Rose says, "Do I have to call you 'doctor'? To me, you're still Daniel."

Daniel smiles. "Rose, to you and Hyman, I will always be Daniel."

Rose says, "So, Doctor Daniel, why'd you come by?"

Daniel says, "When I first left, you said 'come by; you never need a reason to come by.'"

Rose says, "That's true, but you always have a reason."

Daniel takes their hands in his. What he will say will be difficult for them to hear—and difficult for him to say. "I came to tell you that I'm leaving."

Dreading the news that Daniel is going to join the army, Rose says, "Where are you going?"

Daniel sighs before he tells them, "I don't know. I will go wherever they send me. I'm going to enlist."

Rose and Hyman both know what this means. Daniel's decision can lead to him getting hurt or even killed. Rose and Hyman share a look. They had their son, Leon, taken from them so early. They love Daniel like a son, and Rose reacts like a mother. "I don't want this."

Daniel appreciates how much they care about him. "I don't want it either. Nobody wants this, but it's something I have to do."

He hugs them both.

Rose says, "For God's sake, be safe."

"I will do my best."

*

Daniel has a day off every Monday, and for the last few years, he has always spent that day at home. In the morning, he gets ready for Rita. He wants the place neat for her. On Mondays, he transforms it from his apartment to their love nest.

Rita and Ruth trade days to watch the children, and Ruth watches David play with Nathan on Mondays. Rita leaves Nathan and goes to Daniel's. Her step quickens as she hastens to her love. It's routine, glorious routine. They spend most of their time in bed. Occasionally, Rita will bring up the possibility of Daniel finding a wife. Daniel always responds, "I have a wife. It's just that my wife is somebody else's."

Rita bristles at that. "When I am here, I don't think that."

Today's time in bed, after exquisite lovemaking, leaves them exhausted. It is even more intense than it has ever been. They luxuriate in each other's arms. For Daniel, the subject of the impending war hangs over them as it did over Rita and the Shabbat dinner she had with Mikal and his family. Daniel has decided not to be honest with Rita about his decision to enlist.

Finally, Rita breaks open the subject. "On Friday night, Mikal spoke. He doesn't usually speak."

Usually, Daniel is not anxious to hear what Mikal has to say; but this time there is an urgency from Rita, so he asks, "What did he say?"

"He said what we are all thinking—what everyone is thinking about the coming war. It's tearing the family apart. We don't know what is going to happen."

Daniel says, "Nobody does."

The distressed Rita says, "Mikal is too old to go into the army, but his brothers ..."

Daniel is ambiguous when he says, "Everybody has to do what he has to do."

Hearing Rita's anguish about the war confirms for Daniel that he should not tell her he is going to enlist. Though Daniel is concerned about going into the army, it does give him a chance to reconnect with Hoby. They get in touch with each other and make plans to go to the recruiting office at the same time. Hoby tells Daniel that Pat already enlisted in the navy. There are several recruiting offices throughout the city, and Daniel meets Hoby at the one that isn't near the deli or his apartment or the hospital. Besides the fact that he doesn't want to be seen by Rita, those choices would have been too painful and reminders of what he is giving up.

The line inside the recruiting station uptown is as long as it is outside. After an hour, Daniel and Hoby find themselves at the front. The seen-it-all recruiting officer is enlisting as many volunteers as fast as he can, stamping their papers and giving them instructions as to where to go.

While they were in line, Hoby filled Daniel in about his life. How he and Norma have two young children, how this will be a burden on her, but he feels going to fight is his duty. Hoby doesn't know about Daniel's relationship with Rita, or he never would have said, "At least you won't have a woman back home worrying that you might not come back." Oh, if Hoby only knew.

Daniel and Hoby are next in line as the recruiter finishes with the new enlistee in front of them. "Thank you, soldier. Report for your physical on Thursday. Address is on this card."

He hands the card to the soldier, who walks away and is immediately replaced by both Hoby and Daniel. The recruiter is surprised to see two men at the same time in front of him. "It's one at a time."

Hoby speaks for both of them. "We want to go in together."

Shaking his head, the by-the-book recruiter says. "How nice, but it doesn't work that way."

Then he says to Daniel, "You stand over there."

Daniel does as he is directed and moves to the side.

The recruiter addresses Hoby as he has addressed the hundreds of young men that he has seen this day. "Any special skills?"

Hoby is irrepressible. "I can drink anybody under the table."

"Don't be a wise ass. Any skills that the army can use?"

Hoby says something that he believes might change the recruiter's mind about him and Daniel going in together. "No. I'm not like my old friend, Daniel, there. He's a doctor."

The recruiter hears the word doctor and immediately is more interested in Daniel. He says to Hoby, "Now you stand over there. I'm taking your doctor buddy first."

Hoby moves to the side. The recruiter calls to Daniel, "Over here, Doc." Daniel replaces Hoby in front of the recruiter. "You're really a doctor?"

"Yes, I am."

"And you're volunteering?"

"Yes, I want to serve my country."

"And we're happy to have you. Being a doctor, you kind of have your choice on where you want to go."

As Hoby looks on, Daniel says, "Someplace where I can do the most good."

The recruiter says, "You are my kind of doctor."

Hoby nudges Daniel in his back so Daniel can add a caveat to Daniel's request: "And some place where my friend Hoby can go too."

The recruiter recognizes he's in a negotiation. "I get it. I can't promise anything, but I'll do my best."

Then he indicates to both of them: "You'll need to sign these papers."

Daniel, at Hoby's urging, says, "Together?"

The recruiter gives in and confirms, "Together."

Hoby is relieved as Daniel says to the recruiter, "Thank you, friend."

Then the recruiter reverts to form. "Be at the physicals on Thursday. Address is on the card."

Taking their cards, Hoby and Daniel are pleased with themselves. The recruiter calls to the line of men, "If any of you men are doctors, when you get up here, let me know that right away."

*

The war affects everyone. At New World Lights and Lamps, Mikal, Jerome, and two new teenage employees Moshe and Anthony all have champagne as they gather around Willum. Rita and the eight-year-old Nathan are there as well. Because of his having only one hand, Jerome is clearly not someone who is an acceptable recruit, and Moshe and Anthony are too young.

Mikal has everyone's attention. "I should like to propose a toast to Willum. We wish you a safe return from the war. Our prayers are with you. To Willum."

All say, "To Willum," before they drink their champagne. Willum is clearly touched by the gesture of his work family. He is a bit choked up. "I thank you very much. When I volunteered, I was thinking of all of you. Of fighting for the freedom we have in this country. I can't offer the army much. I don't have any special skills, except for selling lamps."

Relieved that he lightened the mood, they all laugh. Rita hugs Mikal as they remember Mikal's brothers who are also going off to the war.

With determination, Willum continues, "But I'll fight and do my best to make you all proud of me."

Rita tells Willum, "We're already proud of you."

Jerome feels a new sense of responsibility and repeats loudly, "To Willum!"

Willum smiles at Jerome and reminds him, "You already toasted me once. Don't you have work?"

Mikal says, "So who said we can't toast you twice? Or even three times. To Willum."

All raise their glasses and repeat what Mikal has suggested. "To Willum."

As all disperse to return to the business of selling lamps, Rita goes to Willum. She has become very fond of their loyal employee/friend. She hugs him. "You come home safe."

Willum appreciates the gesture. "I'll do my best, Mrs. Glass."

With that, Willum musses Nathan's hair and leaves the store to walk out into the unknown. Mikal and Rita share a moment. Mikal says to Rita, "I feel I should be in the fighting."

Rita says, "I don't wish that. Besides, the United States of America says you are too old."

Mikal starts to say, "But still—"

Rita cuts him off. "And the rest of the people at the store need you. And your family needs you."

Rita hugs him. She's proud of his patriotism, but some of her thoughts move to Daniel and where he might be. Could he be going into the service? She and Daniel never talked about it.

Rita takes Nathan on their customary Tuesday walk past the window where he always stands to watch Rita and Nathan pass by. She looks up. He's not there! He's always there. There is no way he would miss it, unless …

CHAPTER SEVENTEEN

It's been almost a year since Daniel enlisted. He sped through basic training with Hoby, and then both were shipped off to France.

In the small village of Cantigny, the army has created a makeshift hospital away from the fighting but near enough to hear the cannon fire. Lying in corners of the ruins of what had been a school, injured men seek pockets of comfort. These men are so lost in their own pain, they barely acknowledge the field medics who bring in their injured comrades on stretchers. The newly wounded are left there as the stretcher-bearers take their stretchers and go off to find others in need of help.

Daniel and Fred, another doctor who works tirelessly to save lives, take soldiers in order of the severity of their wounds. It's both backbreaking and heartbreaking. Just as soon as they can move a man from an operating table, another is brought in to take his place. Fred and Daniel barely look up when an airplane swoops over their triage to drop bombs on the German line, nor do they react when a cannon shell smashes into the small Cantigny church, which had existed since the sixteenth century and now exists only as rubble.

Fred finishes bandaging his latest patient and hardly winces as another shell hits what is left of the church. Fred says to Daniel, who is examining the head wound of his most recent patient, "I thought we already took Cantigny."

Daniel knows enough about the battle to recognize the strategies. "Yes, but now the Germans are counterattacking. Get ready to handle more."

Fred says, "We can barely handle the ones we got."

Daniel turns around to see a medic bring in a soldier who is bandaged around his eyes. By pointing at the man's bandage and shaking his head sadly, the medic indicates that the man is probably blind.

The medic tries to be upbeat when he says, "Another patient for you, Doctor."

Daniel moves to the soldier and says gently, "Hello, friend. Mind if I take a look?"

The bitter blind soldier says, "Do I have a choice?"

Daniel describes what he is doing. "I'm taking off the bandages slowly. They're here to protect your eyes." The soldier grits his teeth out of the fear that he may be blind. As soon as Daniel removes the covering from his eyes, he can see that the soldier is not only blind, but he has also lost both eyes. Daniel makes no sound.

The soldier says, "You're not saying anything."

Daniel says, "My job is to save your life. You can have a productive life. And you get to go home soon."

"My eyes are gone, aren't they?"

"Yes. I'm sorry to say they are."

The soldier laughs at the irony. "And I can't even cry. Will I be able to cry?"

Daniel says, "We're all crying for you. And we're here for you."

Meanwhile, Fred stands near another patient who is lying on an operating table. The soldier has a severe leg injury where he was shot. Fred is about to examine the leg to determine a course of action. Before he pulls the blanket from the soldier, Fred asks, "Can I take a look at your leg?"

The soldier says, "No."

Fred says, "If I can't look, I can't help you,"

The soldier says, "You can look if you promise you won't cut off my leg."

Fred says, "I can't make that promise."

The soldier grimaces and whimpers loudly from the pain.

Fred says, "Now will you let me help you?"

The soldier gives up and says, "Go ahead."

Very gently, Fred pulls back the blanket. He has seen many broken legs, many shattered legs that can't be repaired and knows the difference. Fred would only consider amputation as a last resort. The soldier wants to know Fred's opinion, even if it's something the soldier doesn't want to hear. "If you're going to cut it off, knock me out first."

Fred says, "That I can promise."

With further examination, Fred is satisfied he has better news for the soldier. "You're going to keep the leg."

The soldier starts to cry with happiness. "Thanks, Doc. Thanks."

As Fred cleans the wound, he adds, "But you will have a pretty big limp."

The soldier is able to smile. "Get me on a boat, and when I hit the states, I'll limp all the way back to Milwaukee."

Daniel needs to take a breather, a break from the grueling work. As he steps outside, two soldiers carry in a body on a stretcher. Daniel has seen many bodies, many deaths, but something catches his eye. He moves to this particular stretcher where he sees an arm dangling from underneath the blanket. One of the soldiers says, "You won't be able to help this one, Doc. Half of him is missing."

Daniel had spotted what looked like Hoby's distinct ring, though he hopes against hope that it's not his friend. As the soldiers put down the body, Daniel pulls back the blanket and sees that it is indeed the maimed body of Hoby. Daniel hardly reacts since, by now, he is drained of emotion. He has seen too many injuries, too many deaths. Daniel had known Hoby since college, and now he's gone. He just stares at Hoby's body. This death is way too personal. He turns to one of the stretcher-bearers, "Do you know how he died?"

The stretcher-bearer sees the dog tag and says, "They say Ellman, and his unit was—"

Daniel cuts him off. "Call him Hoby."

"Then you knew him?"

"Yes."

"They say that Hoby's unit was trapped in a ravine. They were being shot at from above. The only way to get out was to fight their way to the top. Hoby stood up and yelled at the others: 'Come on. Follow me. Or we'll never get our asses out of here.' Then he ran up the hill. Everyone followed. They made it. They got out. But at the top … that's when he was blasted."

Daniel says, "Thanks. Thanks for telling me. It sounds like Hoby."

Daniel thinks that maybe if he and Hoby hadn't made a pact to be in the same place, Hoby wouldn't be dead now, but Daniel won't let himself believe that. The stretcher-bearers don't see Daniel slip Hoby's ring from his finger and put it in his pocket. Then Daniel talks to Hoby as if Hoby were still alive. "Hoby, before you go, you need to know how much you were loved—by me, by Pat, and especially your family. When I get back, I'll check in with Norma. God bless you and keep you, Hoby."

*

Daniel had just disappeared. He wasn't in the window for a few weeks. Getting in touch with Rita was always hit or miss. Then one day, the phone rang during the day when Mikal was at work. She answers and says, "Hello."

It is Daniel. In Russian, he said, *"It's better this way."* And then he hangs up.

"Better this way?" He couldn't mean that. Then, no communication from him for a year. A year that became unendurable for Rita. She can't get Daniel out of her mind and her heart. She goes to his hospital. She thinks that Daniel spends so much time here and talks about it so much that she should know exactly where to go to see him.

However, Rita is disoriented. She only knows the hospital from looking up to Daniel's window from the street. She walks to the hospital information desk where Agnes, the cheerful hospital volunteer, is ready to answer any questions and to point visitors in the right direction. Rita speaks softly, "Hello."

Obviously, Rita is not in need of medical help. Agnes assumes, "Do you need to know a patient's room number?"

Rita responds, "Actually no. My name is Rita Glass. I'm looking for a doctor."

"This is a hospital. You have come to the right place."

Rita says, "I mean a specific doctor: Daniel Stabinski."

Agnes says, "Doctor Stabinski is no longer at the hospital."

Rita stares at Agnes. She can't believe what Agnes has just told her. "What?"

"He left us to serve in the army."

Rita now realizes why Daniel was so distant the last time they were together and why he said what he said on the phone call to her. But he left without an explanation. How could he do that? Why would he do that? Agnes sees that Rita is upset by the news that Daniel isn't here. She asks Rita, "Is Dr. Stabinski a friend of yours?"

That snaps Rita out of her contemplations. "Yes."

"What's your name again?"

"Rita Glass."

The name echoes for Agnes, and she tells Rita, "Give me a minute. I want to check something." Agnes opens a drawer in the desk and pulls out a file. She checks names and then tells Rita, "Oh, yes. Your name is right here."

Rita is surprised. "What? My name is where?"

As if to prove what she discovered, Agnes shows Rita what she has found. "Right here. Dr. Stabinski lists: 'Rita Glass' as his next of kin."

This stuns Rita. All she can get out is a gasp. The sympathetic Agnes says, "I guess you didn't know."

"No. No, I didn't. But thank you. Thank you for telling me."

Agnes observes, "We both know Dr. Stabinski. I'm sure he didn't tell you he was going into the army because he didn't want to worry you. That's how he is: always thinking of others."

"Yes. That's right."

As the numbed Rita leaves the hospital, Agnes looks at Rita's name in the Dr. Stabinski file once again before she puts it away.

CHAPTER EIGHTEEN

Between battles, sometimes doctors are pulled from the fighting lines so they can provide medical assistance to civilians who have been injured. When this happens, Daniel is then given lodging in an inn or a hotel. In this French town of Grivesnes, Daniel can also be alone with his thoughts while aiding the citizenry. He's in a lobby/bar of his lodging as social activity whirls around him. It's as if the people of the town go about their normal life in order to black out the horror of the war. Some soldiers mix with the French townspeople. Some soldiers do more than mix and find prostitutes to take their minds off the fighting. Daniel has found a corner of the room where he writes letters. He writes some letters in English; some in Russian. Fred has a French companion for the evening, but he stops by Daniel on his way upstairs with Yvette.

Fred urges Daniel, "Come on, Dan, I've got Yvette, but there are plenty more to choose from. They can clear your head and your body. God knows we've earned it."

Daniel has turned down Fred before. Fred expects it, but maybe Daniel will change his mind this time. Daniel doesn't judge Fred. Each to his own. He tells Fred, "That's all right. You go ahead."

Fred gives it one more try. "Not that Yvette understands English, but she is not paid to be a good listener."

Fred points out another willing prostitute. "Look at Chantal. She's different than the bodies we've been seeing all day. She's in one piece and not dead."

Daniel appreciates what Fred is trying to do. He isn't interested. He tells Fred, "You go ahead. I've got some writing to do."

Now with his hand brazenly on Yvette's chest, Fred leads her to the stairway. He says to Daniel, "Suit yourself. You have your kind of fun. I'll have mine."

Daniel turns to his writing. *"Dear Rita. This is the start of my second month here, and it gives me comfort to write to you, to know that you are there for me, in my heart. It keeps me going in the midst of all the horror of what I have seen. I said goodbye to Hoby today. You remember him. I've written to you about him before. He was one of my oldest friends in America. Hoby is going home, but not to a welcome. He's going home to the tears of a family who loved him and will now only have memories to hold on to where he, himself, should have been."*

He pauses before he begins to write more.

*

At Greenbaum's Delicatessen, Hyman is at the counter as usual. The last customer of the day finishes paying for her order. He gives her change. 'Here's fifteen cents back. Thank you, Mrs. Weisbaum."

She clutches her bag. "And thank you, Mr. Greenbaum."

As she goes out, he says to her, "Enjoy the knishes. Fresh today."

Before he puts out the closed sign, he turns back as Rose comes out of the back room. She has an impish smile. Hyman sees her grin. "I know that smile. That smile says we got another letter from Daniel."

"What can I say? You know me, Hyman."

"Did you read it?"

"Would I read it without you? Come."

They go into the back room where a bulletin board is loaded with tacked-up letters from Daniel. They sit at a table where Hyman and Rose read the letter together.

"Dear beloved friends. Writing to both of you makes the days go by more quickly. I have told the other doctors and some patients about you and the deli. I may have bragged too much, so when this war is over, you will probably get a lot more customers. If they mention they know Dr. Stabinski, give them some money off. They have earned it because of what all of us are going through over here. I love you, and I miss you. Your Daniel."

Hyman and Rose say a silent prayer for the safety of their honorary son, then they take the letter and pin it next to the many on the bulletin board.

*

Rita is in the kitchen of their home. She is washing some dishes, putting others away, but mostly she is listening to what Mikal and Nathan are talking about in the other room. Mikal is reading a newspaper account of the war. Mikal tells Nathan, "That's all the news today. The Battle of the Marne."

Nathan is filled with curiosity. "Is the Marne in France?"

Mikal says, "That's right."

Nathan asks, "Is that where Uncle Josef and Uncle Sid are?"

"The last letters we got from them said they were in England."

In the other room, Rita thinks that she has no idea where Daniel is.

Nathan points to a sentence in the paper, "What's this word?"

Mikal says, "Which word?"

Nathan tries to pronounce the word he is pointing at, "Cas-yu-al-tees."

Mikal says softly, "Oh, that word is casualties."

Nathan does his best to make sense out of the sentences as he reads awkwardly. "It says casualties are high, more so among the German forces than the Allies. France suffered 95,000 casualties, Germany 168,000, Britain incurring 13,000 losses, and the United States 12,000."

Then Nathan says, "I don't understand."

Mikal feels he must be honest with Nathan. "Casualties are men who are injured or have died in the battles."

"Are Uncle Josef and Uncle Sid casualties?"

Rita enters to join the discussion. "We hope and pray not. We have not heard that. We hope and pray that no one we know is a casualty."

Nathan instinctively hugs Mikal, happy that Mikal is in the house and not overseas where he could be a casualty. Mikal senses the boy's fear. "That's okay. I'm here."

Nathan says, "There are a lot of casualties."

Rita says, "Too many. One is one too many."

But Mikal brightens the mood. He points to another article. "But there is good news. Right here it says that the war is almost over."

Rita adds, "Thank God. Maybe the men can come home soon."

Nathan says, "Like Uncle Josef and Uncle Sid?"

Mikal says, "And Willum."

Rita says, "Right. Like Willum."

She may have said the name Willum, but she certainly thinks of Daniel even more than Willum.

Nathan says, "Isn't that the best news?"

Rita certainly agrees. "Yes. Yes, it is."

*

In a French tent city, when news of the armistice arrives, pent-up joy explodes as the Great War has ended. Music from squeezeboxes, flutes, and guitars has the soldiers dancing with themselves or French women eager to carouse as all celebrate the end of hostilities. Pictures and drawings of the German enemy are defaced to show their animosity. "Down with the Kaiser, the Hun is dead!"

"November 11, 1911, Armistice Day!"

Fred is as drunk as a skunk. He tries to pour more wine in tankards for two equally drunk soldiers. He misses, but some goes in, while most splashes out, and no one cares since some wine is better than none. They toast Fred when one says, "To you, Doc. Happy I never needed you."

As before, Daniel isn't part of socializing. He sits on a chair and uses a lantern for light, and he uses a trunk as a makeshift desk.

Fred finishes his latest drink and staggers over to Daniel. "C'mon, Daniel. Put your pen down. Tonight, you have some fun."

Daniel looks over at the revelry. It's nothing he wants to participate in. He tells Fred, "I'm having fun."

Not to be dissuaded this time, Fred takes the letter from his friend's hand and tries to read it. "Hey, what language is this?"

"Russian."

Then Daniel grabs it back. Even though Fred can't read a word, the fact that he is looking at it is a sacrilege for Daniel.

Fred backs off. "You know, Daniel, you write all those letters, but these Russian ones you never put them in the mail sack to be picked up."

Daniel is elusive when he says, "That's right."

Daniel is not making sense—not to Fred, anyway. "But how do you send them?"

"I don't mail these letters."

With that, Fred watches as Daniel takes the letter he has been writing and opens his trunk. This letter is added to a stack of unsent letters in Russian on top of his belongings.

Fred says, "I may be drunk, but let me get this straight: While I have been out every night getting three sheets to the wind, you have been writing all these letters in Russian that you don't send?"

Daniel says, "Not exactly right. I do write letters in English to my friends Hyman and Rose Greenbaum, which I do send."

"Doing it this way got you through the war?"

"Yes."

Running back to the join the gaiety, Fred calls back, "You got through your way, and I got through mine." As if to prove it, Fred grabs the first woman he can find and gives her a passionate kiss. Then he lets her go so he can kiss another woman.

CHAPTER NINETEEN

Every other Thursday, Mikal asks the employees of New World Lights and Lamps to stay late to go over receipts and inventory and delivery schedules. Then he takes them all for a piece of cake at Rosenberg's, the local restaurant.

Rita looks forward to those evenings since she uses the time for a secret activity. After Rita puts Nathan to bed, she goes into her room and then her closet. She removes the last drawer of her dresser. Underneath that drawer is the diary she has been writing. This is where she can share the story of her life and her innermost thoughts. She has been writing in her diary ever since the day before she got married. All of it is in Russian, and she discloses whatever has happened and what her mood happens to be. Obviously, Mikal doesn't know of the diary's existence. It would surprise him and disappoint him greatly since much of it is about Daniel. No, this is just for her. This is where she can be truthful about her feelings and her love for Daniel. It's also a place where she can describe how her double life troubles her. For now, as she writes in her diary, she gives no thought that someday somebody might read this. No, it's just for her in just the place where she can be herself.

*

Every troop ship arriving in New York Harbor is cause for celebration. Crowds pour out into the streets. It's as if each person wants to be the first to find the soldier who he or she is dying to embrace with all the love they have been storing up for that moment. And not just family who are rushing to the docks. Grateful Americans want to be part of the homecomings.

Rita walks with Nathan hurriedly down the sidewalk to join many equally rushing walkers who practically break into running. Nathan's legs are shorter and have difficulty keeping up with Rita, who urges him to stay up with her.

"Come, Nathan, we don't want to be late."

Nathan doesn't understand where everyone is rushing. "Mom, you didn't even tell me where we're going."

"The ships are coming in!"

"What ships?"

As they dodge through many people to get there quickly, she tells him, "The troopships. We are good Americans. We need to go down and wave to the soldiers to show them we appreciate them, that we're happy they're home." She takes two small American flags from her bag and hands one to Nathan. "Here. Wave this, so they'll see you."

The boy enjoys waving his flag when they find themselves in an ever-increasing sea of equally excited friends and relatives of the returning soldiers. They swarm down to the dock and see a huge ship brought in by harbor tugboats. Every soldier is on deck. As excited as the crowd is to see them come home, they are more excited to make it back alive and victorious while anxious to leave behind the war with its bloodstained, painful memories. The waving soldiers are met with cheers and music from the band on the dock. Everybody is crying. Even the band misses notes because they are so caught up in the emotion.

Rita and Nathan search in a desperate hope that someone they know will see them. Rita tells Nathan, "Wave, Nathan, wave!"

Rita waves her flag, and Nathan waves his enthusiastically. As he does, he asks, "There are so many soldiers. Who am I waving at?"

Rita knows who she wants to see when she tells her son, "Pick somebody. Pick anybody. Just wave to say that you're glad he's home. Maybe somebody will see you."

He waves even more vigorously. "Like Uncle Josef and Uncle Sid?"

"That's right."

"Like Mr. Van Hoff?"

"Yes."

Meanwhile, Rita scours the faces of the soldiers, hoping against all odds that she'll see Daniel. Nathan continues to wave; she continues to try to find Daniel among the thousands of faces aboard this one ship.

*

That evening at the kitchen table, Mikal, Rita, and Nathan are eating dinner. Rita doesn't say anything about where they were. Nathan says to his mother, "Are you going to tell Poppa where we were today?"

This piques Mikal's interest. "Where? Where did you go? Ruth and David's?"

Nathan answers, "No. That's where we go every day. Today, we went down to the dock to wave at the soldiers."

This news takes Mikal by surprise. Rita hadn't mentioned that was what they were going to do. "You were?"

Rita tells him, "Yes, we were."

Nathan is proud of where they had been. "Mom said we should greet them because they were so brave."

Mikal asks, "Did you see your uncles? Did you see Willum?"

Nathan says, "I kept waving my flag, but I couldn't tell anybody from anybody."

Rita adds, "We don't know if any of them were even on that ship."

Mikal says, "I'm proud of both of you. That was a very good thing to do. Very proud."

*

In uniform, Daniel pauses a moment before he enters the hospital. He thought it would look different, but it doesn't. It looks exactly the same. It's as if the two years he spent overseas had never happened. How could that be? How could the world be changed but unchanged? He moves into the lobby area. Agnes still works at the information/registration desk. She is talking to a visitor who is asking if there are any places nearby to buy flowers. Agnes is pointing out the door when she sees Daniel walk in.

Even in his uniform, she recognizes him instantly. "Oh, my God!"

The visitor is startled, and even more startled when the receptionist comes out from behind the desk and moves quickly to Daniel, who she embraces. "Dr. Stabinski!"

The visitor grasps what is happening and passes the hugging Agnes and Daniel. He says, "I guess I can find it myself." He leaves.

Agnes gushes to Daniel, "I am so happy you're back."

"Trust me, Agnes, I'm even happier than you are."

"And look at you in your uniform."

Daniel tells her, "I can't wait to get back into my white doctor coat."

They walk further into the hospital. Agnes wants to know everything, starting with, "How long have you been back?"

"Just a day."

Then Daniel is surprised and disconcerted when Agnes asks, "Have you seen Rita Glass yet?"

This question catches Daniel by surprise. "What?"

She repeats the name, but Agnes can tell by his reaction that she may have been a little too prying. Daniel covers his emotion. "I don't know what you're talking about."

Agnes tells him what she remembers about the day Rita came to the hospital and explains, "I was at the desk here when a lady named Rita Glass came in while you were overseas. She was asking about you. I looked in your file and found her name there."

Daniel says, "What did you tell her?"

Agnes says, "That you wrote her down as your next of kin. Did I do something wrong?"

"No."

Agnes can't resist subtly pressing for more information and says, "She is a very attractive woman."

Daniel fails at being nonchalant. "I know that."

"Are you seeing her?"

Daniel tries to end any more questioning. "No. She is just somebody I knew once. That's in the past."

Agnes knows when she has crossed the line. "Whatever you say." Then she changes subjects, something that Daniel is pleased about. "What was it like over there?"

"Agnes, nobody should ever know what it was like. The pain we see in the hospital is nothing compared to the horror of that war. How can man do that to man? May it never happen again."

Agnes says, "God willing." Then she suggests, "Now, I suppose you want to take some time off."

That's the last thing Daniel wants. He wants to retrieve some semblance of his life. How does the fact that Rita knows he wrote down Rita as his next of kin figure into his life? He doesn't know. There are too many questions to which he has no answers. One thing at a time. And none of it is something to discuss with Agnes, the hospital receptionist.

He says to her. "No. I want to get back to work right away. Is Dr. Gethers in?"

"I think he's in his office."

As he heads toward the hospital chief's office, he tosses back to Agnes, "Good. I want to report for duty—I mean tell him I'm back."

*

Nathan and David are at Ruth's house playing with toy soldiers on the floor. David asks Nathan, "How come you didn't come here yesterday?"

Nathan is proud to answer, "Me and my mom went down to the pier to wave to the ships and the soldiers."

David is jealous and yells out to Ruth, who is talking with Rita in the kitchen, "Mom, why didn't we go?"

Ruth responds, "Why didn't we go where?"

David calls back, "Nathan and his mom went to wave at the ships and the soldiers. Why didn't we go?"

Ruth answers, "I don't know. Maybe because we don't know any soldiers."

Satisfied with the answer, David continues playing with Nathan.

In the kitchen, Ruth and Rita have their own conversation as Ruth asks Rita, "Did you see anybody you knew?"

Rita says, "No. We were looking for Mikal's brothers and somebody from Mikal's store."

Ruth says, "So that's who you were waving at?"

Rita is evasive. "More or less. Can I have some water?"

"Sure."

As Rita gets a glass and takes tap water, Ruth senses that there is something Rita is not telling her. "You can't say 'more or less' and leave it like that."

Now Ruth knows Rita is hiding something when Rita says, "Can we not talk about it?"

Ruth tells her friend, "You can't just say, 'Can we not talk about it?' and not talk about it. Who's your best friend?"

Rita realizes the truth is about to come out. In some ways, she is relieved that finally there will be someone to talk to about Daniel. Rita makes the decision to confide in Ruth. "You are." Rita casts a glance toward the room where Nathan and David are playing. By that gesture, Ruth understands that she is about to hear something from Rita that will change or deepen the relationship between the two women.

Rita realizes it too, but there is no turning back. "If I tell you, you have to promise that for as long as we live, you won't tell anybody else—ever."

Ruth sees how profoundly serious her friend is and responds in kind. "I promise."

"Even though he probably wasn't going to be there, I was looking for a particular soldier on the ship. Someone I knew very well."

"How well?"

"Very well."

Ruth doesn't need Rita to fill in the rest of the story, not yet anyway. For now, she asks Rita, "Does Mikal know about him?"

Rita, herself, doesn't know everything. She tells Ruth, "Mikal has met him, but Mikal doesn't know everything."

Now both women look to where their sons are playing.

Then Ruth asks, "What's his name?"

Once she says the name, Rita cements the fact that Ruth and she will have a secret that will bind them forever.

She says softly, "Daniel Stabinski. He's a doctor."

"And was he on the ship?"

"I don't know. I don't think so. I would like to believe he was and that he's home safely."

"If he's home, do you want to see him?"

Rita mentally goes through the ramifications if she continues with Daniel before she answers Ruth honestly, "I don't know."

Ruth tries to follow her friend's logic. "But you went there?"

Rita doesn't have to be reminded. "I know."

"Why?"

Rita knows why. In a whisper, she says, "Because I love him."

Ruth embraces her troubled friend.

*

Daniel is neither in his uniform nor his doctor coat but just in street clothes when he steps through the front door of the deli. He takes a moment to inhale the welcome smells that were always there and are there still. Hyman hasn't seen him yet. And Daniel likes that. He can just watch Hyman scurrying about to clean off the slicer and the counter between taking orders from customers. Then, as if he knows he is being watched, Hyman looks up and sees Daniel. Hyman doesn't move. He just starts to cry tears of joy. He doesn't greet Daniel. He just yells out, "Rose!"

Then, as Hyman moves to Daniel, Rose comes out of the back room. Hyman's yell was the kind of emotional yell she hadn't heard before. She hasn't yet seen Daniel when she answers, "What's the matter?" Now she sees Daniel and breaks into the same sobs that mirror how her husband feels. Customers see the moment among these three. They understand immediately.

Daniel is embarrassed. He says, "Now I know you care about me."

Between tears, Rose says, "Was there a doubt?"

Daniel says, "No. And I love you for that."

When the deli closes for the day, Daniel, Hyman, and Rose spend the entire evening together. Daniel tells them everything, from the day he enlisted to the terror of the battlefield. He doesn't go into detail about the death and pain, but he tells them how he felt being there trying to save as many as he could. He tells them how much he missed them. Daniel has never talked so much in his life. Rose keeps filling his coffee cup as Daniel's reflections come pouring out of him in no particular order. As he speaks, Hyman and Rose are filled with relief as well as the pride they have in Daniel.

*

There is one more necessary place that Daniel must visit. He finds himself in Hoboken where he looks for Norma's address. He finds the small house where Hoby and she had settled. Daniel looks through the window into the living room where he sees Norma's two young daughters playing with dolls. Daniel moves to the front door and knocks. Inside, Norma isn't expecting anyone. She opens the door and sees Daniel. She is surprised and happy to see him. "Daniel? What are you doing here?"

She hugs him warmly. Daniel tries to lighten the mood. "I was in the neighborhood."

Norma knows that isn't the truth. "Nobody just happens to be in Hoboken. Come in."

He steps in and stops in the doorway. Norma turns to the two little girls. "Girls, this is your daddy's and my old friend, Daniel." They nod and are not impressed. They'd much prefer to keep playing with their dolls.

Daniel says about the girls, "They're so cute."

Norma says, "Just like Hoby to end up with two girls."

She takes him through the living room and into the kitchen. "If I knew you were coming…"

"I didn't want you to know. I wanted to surprise you."

"Well, you did a good job." Norma has some coffee on the stove and pours him a cup. "Cream? Sugar?"

He declines both.

Norma is glad to have the company, especially someone who was close to Hoby. She speaks in a rush. "I knew so little about what happened. It just came as a telegram. A cold telegram. 'We regret to inform you.' That's all I read for a while. I thought if I didn't finish reading it, it wouldn't be true. But it was. Do you know any more than that?"

"I know what they told me."

"Tell me."

Daniel takes a breath. He knows it will be hard for Norma to hear, but he also knows that Hoby's widow should know as much as he knows. "They said Hoby's unit was trapped in a ravine. Shots were coming from up top. The only way to get out was to fight their way to the top. Hoby stood up and yelled at the others: 'Come on. Follow me. Or we'll never get our asses out of here!' They said he ran up the hill. Everyone followed.

They made it. They got out. But at the top … that's when he was shot. He was a hero."

Then Daniel is careful to find the right words to tell her about seeing Hoby that last time. "I wasn't with him when he was killed. I am a doctor, and I was in a makeshift hospital when they brought him in."

"So, you saw him?"

"Yes."

"Did he talk to you? Did he say anything?"

"I'm so sorry. No. He was already gone. But I talked to him. I told him how much we all loved him."

She breaks down. "Oh, thank you. Thank you."

"And I told him I would see you."

Daniel reaches into his pocket and produces Hoby's ring, the ring he had taken from Hoby's finger before his friend was taken away. He hands it to her silently. They both cry. The two little girls look up from their playing when they hear the weeping from their mother and the man who came into the house.

CHAPTER TWENTY

For the first few days at the hospital, Daniel is preoccupied. His mind is not flashing back to the time in the war. No, his thoughts turn to Rita while he tries to decide what to do about her. True, he made her his next of kin. And he knows she knows that. He also knows how much he loves her, and he knows she loves him. While he tries to concentrate on patients and his hospital responsibilities, he can't control what his heart feels. He knows he must contact her to let her know he is back. He knows that is important to her.

But after that? He is just not sure. He'll rely on their old system. He hopes that she will too. They always had an unspoken special kind of communication. If that is true, she will walk by the hospital on Tuesday at 3:30 with Nathan. And he'll be in the window to wave. She'll see him, and she'll know that he's back and alive. And it will give him a chance to see Nathan. On Tuesday, Daniel finishes going over a chart with Sophie, a nurse at the nurse's station. "Sophie, give Mr. Levy his medication right after he eats his afternoon meal."

"Yes, Doctor."

Daniel looks at his watch: 3:20. Enough time to get to his office. He is nervous. Will they be there? And if not, what can he do? What should he do?

Rita and Nathan walk down the sidewalk. Nathan is surprised that they are taking this route. They hadn't for a while. Nathan says, "This way? We haven't walked this way for a long time."

Rita tells her son, "I know. I just thought we'd try it again."

Nathan shrugs. He really doesn't care which way they walk. They pass by the hospital. She hopes that Daniel will be there. She looks up toward Daniel's office window. She sees him. She gasps when she sees him in the window waving. It's Daniel. Daniel! Her heart jumps. Thank God. He's back and he's safe.

Nathan reacts to Rita's gasp. "Mom, are you all right?"

Rita says, "I'm fine. I just had to catch my breath."

Luckily, he doesn't question her anymore since she wouldn't know what to invent.

After Daniel sees Rita and Nathan, he turns away from the window. He's made contact with her. And he is just as emotional about it as she is. Are they picking up where they left off? He doesn't know. It would make sense not to; it would be easier not to. But for Daniel, nothing about their relationship has made sense or been easy.

*

It's the first Shabbat dinner since Mikal's brothers have both returned from the war. Rita wants to make it special, and she spends all day preparing the meal. She has even bought new plates for the occasion. Mikal comes home early from work to help, and he tries to stay out of the way. He mostly assists Rita by keeping Nathan from being in the way. "Come, Nathan, tell me what happened in school today."

"There was a spelling test, and I only missed one."

"Which one? See if I can spell it."

"Orange."

"That's a hard word. I don't even think I can spell it."

"Try."

Mikal deliberately gets it wrong. "O – R – E – N – J – E."

Nathan laughs. "You spelled it even worse than I did. O – R – A –N – G – E."

Rita stops laying out the silverware to look at her son and husband. Their closeness is obvious and something that Rita cherishes. While she is lost in the moment, the door opens, and the guests spill into the room. Rita sees them and calls out, "Mikal, would you and Nathan take everybody's coats while I finish getting the table ready?"

That's what Mikal and Nathan do. It's a little more difficult since Mikal's brother lost a leg in the war. Josef is on crutches. This is the first time Nathan has seen his uncle without two legs. Josef catches him staring at his empty pantleg. Josef says, "Nathan, I'm back. I left the other leg over there. They can have it."

Everyone migrates to the dinner table, and compliments fly as they say how festive the house looks, how the delicious aromas from the kitchen waft in. Rita appreciates their appreciation. Before the actual dinner, Rita lights the candles and says the prayer.

"Bah-rookh ah-tah ah-doh-noi eh-loh-hay-noo meh-lekh hah-oh-lahm ah-sher ki-deh-shah-noo beh-mitz-voh-tahv veh-tzee-vah-noo leh-hahd-lik nehr shehl shah-baht."

She looks up as the gathered family says, "Amen." As before, she looks at Mikal and Nathan, and their close bond affects her. Before they start dinner, Josef says, "Can I speak?"

Looks all around. This is unusual and a break from tradition. All look toward the head of the family, Mikal, who says, "Of course."

Josef stands, and his wife, Rivka, holds his arm to support him as he says what he wants to say. "I am talking for Sid too. When we were over there, both of us were more worried about the family than we were worried about the fighting. We didn't have to worry at all since Mikal was here. He is the best brother, and we want to say how much we love him and Rita and what they did to make things easier for everyone while we were gone. Not only did he pay all the rent, but he also took care of any bills. And he took care of the family too, the whole family."

All eyes go to Mikal, who modestly says, "You both did the hard part."

Then Rivka taps Josef's crutch and adds, "And he arranged for us to move to the first floor of the building."

Then when Rivka helps Josef ease back into his chair, Rita's mother stands.

She rarely...if ever...talks. In fact, she has never even learned English. She speaks in Russian and says, *"We all know that Mikal is a good brother and a good uncle and a good husband and a good father. My Abraham chose wisely when he picked Mikal for our Rita. We never had a son, but sometimes I think that Mikal is my son."*

Mikal kisses her. Rita can't agree more with the sentiments. She is grateful for what she has and for what a special person Mikal is.

*

Ever since Daniel saw Rita and Nathan, and for the next few days, Daniel had trouble concentrating. He is checking the breathing of a patient when he is interrupted by a nurse who tells him that the hospital administrator, Dr. Gethers, wants to see him. Daniel finishes seeing one more patient before he goes to Dr. Gethers's office. Daniel has always been considered the best doctor at the hospital, so that is why the conversation is difficult for Dr. Gethers. "Dr. Stabinski, I have never taken the time to officially welcome you back from the war."

Daniel responds, "We have both been so busy, and I wanted to get right back to work."

"I know. And that's what the staff told me. Which brings me to the other reason I needed to see you."

From Dr. Gethers's tone, Daniel suspects that whatever Dr. Gethers is about to say won't be pleasant.

"Dr. Stabinski, do you think you rushed getting back? I won't tell you who, but more than one person has reported you seem distracted. You prescribed a medication that we don't even have here. Something that is only used to treat shrapnel wounds."

"I'm sorry."

"It's not a matter of being sorry. Do you think you need a little more time before you come back to us?"

"No. I will do better. I promise."

Dr. Gethers has to make a decision. Recognizing the determination in Daniel's voice, the hospital chief says, "I trust you, Dr. Stabinski. You have always had impeccable judgment. Welcome back."

Daniel is relieved. "No. Thank you, Dr. Gethers."

Daniel leaves the office. On the way back to treat more patients, he knows that he is distracted because he has been thinking about Rita.

That night, Daniel is in his apartment. He is cooking his dinner when there is a knock at the door. He turns off the stove and moves through his living room. He hopes that it is Rita, since hardly anyone, except for her, visits him at home. When he gets to the door and opens it, it is indeed Rita.

She had told Mikal she was going to visit her mother, but she came here, here to be with Daniel. They stand there looking at each other, staring at each other. It has been a long time since they have been together, but for some reason, now neither knows what to say. They have so much to say that they don't even know where to start. She breaks into tears. Are they tears of joy since he has returned safely? That's part of it, but there is more. He hugs her close to him. She allows him to envelop her in his arms.

He says, "You don't have to talk."

She whispers, "Thank you."

Then he takes her hand and leads her through his living room and toward his bedroom. As they move, he tells her everything he has been thinking. "You are what got me through. You are all I thought about. I was helping to save lives, putting men back together ... but even while I was doing that, you were with me ... in my heart. In my soul."

Now they are in the bedroom, and he continues to talk while he undresses her. She is barely conscious of the fact that she has allowed him to strip her of her clothing. It feels totally natural and appropriate.

He continues to talk as he removes his own clothes and eases her to the bed. "Each day became the next and filled with what I had to do to get by, but night—that was our time. I would remember the times we were together, both in Ukraine and here. And then I'd write you about it all."

What? She never saw any letters. "I didn't get any mail from you."

"I didn't send any of them. I still have them. If I sent them, someone else could read them, and that wouldn't be good for us. No, sometime when we are with each other forever, we will read them together."

She starts to cry again. He holds her. At first, he embraces her to comfort her, and then the mood changes to intimacy. They are kissing, and then touching each other tenderly, then passionately. Daniel dreamt of the moment Rita would be back in his arms and in his bed. They can't get enough of each other, and she matches his intensity. He possesses her, and she is willing to be possessed until they are both spent.

They lie still in each other's arms for several minutes. Then Daniel teases her a little, "This is when you usually say, 'I have to get back.'"

"I can't leave yet. Because once I leave—"

Something about the way she says that alerts Daniel that Rita has gotten serious. He says to her, "What is it? We've always been able to talk about everything."

She cups his face in her hands. "Daniel, I love you. I always will."

"And I love you, but what are you trying to say?"

"I needed to know you were well. I needed to see you one last time. To love you like we did one last time."

"One last time? That's not what I want. I want you. I want you forever."

"And I want you. That's what makes this so hard. Our son knows only one father. As careful as we are, we could be discovered. What would that do to Nathan? We can't risk turning his life upside down. I wouldn't want that. I couldn't want that. And if you love me, and if you love your son, you won't want that either."

"You want me to just walk away from you? After all this time?"

"No. That's not what I want. But that's what it has to be."

Daniel says, "I love you."

"I know that. God, I know that. I will love you forever."

"You know what I told you a long time ago. I will always love you."

Their talk has left them both exhausted. They lie embracing. They know it's for the last time, and neither can bear it.

CHAPTER TWENTY-ONE

The next few years are painful for Daniel and Rita. For several weeks, Rita would still walk Nathan by the hospital, but Daniel stopped waiting for them at his window as he used to. It's not that he doesn't care. It's the exact opposite. It would be too painful for him to continue to see her and Nathan.

After a while, Rita doesn't walk by with Nathan anymore. She knows how seeing them would hurt Daniel. Although Daniel and Rita don't get together, they are never out of each other's thoughts. If anything, their voluntary separation makes their feelings for each other grow even deeper.

The Jewish community in lower Manhattan is a close one. News rockets from street to street. It doesn't take long for Daniel, via the Jewish grapevine, to learn that thirteen-year-old Nathan's bar mitzvah ceremony is upcoming. According to Jewish tradition, Nathan will be a man. For Daniel, how could it possibly be that long? But then again, so much has gone on. For Daniel. For Rita. For Mikal. For Nathan. For the world. Yes, Nathan will be celebrating another milestone without the father he only met once.

Daniel determines to be at the ceremony—at least part of the ceremony. The brick synagogue housing Congregation Rodeph Sholom has been presenting bar mitzvah services since the day it opened its doors in the middle of the 1800s. Mikal and Rita and the families of Mikal's brothers are all members of the congregation, as is Rita's mother.

Rabbi Horowitz, who officiated at Rita's father's funeral, presides over the bar mitzvah. All the people whom Mikal and Rita hold dear are in attendance. Family and friends include Ruth and David and Ruth's husband, Aaron.

Mikal has invited all his employees from New World Lights and Lamp. Many of them have never been in a synagogue before. Their eyes wander from the service to focus on the stained-glass windows, the ark, the rich carpeting, then back to the cantor and the rabbi singing and speaking in a language they don't understand. But the melodies are hauntingly beautiful, and they enjoy seeing Mikal, Rita, and Nathan in front of them on the bema.

Nathan has been attending Hebrew school for years. He begins the prayer for his portion of the Torah. *"Baruch atah, Adonai, Eloheinu, Melech haolam, asher bachar bin;vi-im tovim, v'ratzah v'divreihem hane-emarim be-emet."*

"Baruch atah, Adonai, habocher ba Torah uv'Moshe, avdo, uv'Yisrael amo, uvin'-ei ha-emet vatzedek."

Daniel stands outside the temple and listens. He waits nearby in a small grove of trees, trees that remind him of the trees on the hill back in Bukachivtski where he and Rita used to go many years ago. Daniel knows the ceremony well enough. At a certain point, everyone will be looking at Nathan, who will be doing a long recitation. This is the perfect time for Daniel to sneak in without being seen. He can be inconspicuous in the back row of the congregation. Daniel stands at the rear of the synagogue. Nathan continues, and Daniel looks at him and gains an appreciation of the young man his son is becoming.

Behind Nathan and next to the cantor are Rita and Mikal. Rita watches with pride as Nathan recites his Haftorah. She looks beautiful and proud. As if she knows Daniel would be there, she looks up and spies him at the rear of the temple. Their eyes meet. She nods in silent approval that he has come.

Daniel leaves without anyone else being conscious that he was there at all.

Daniel returns home, and this brownstone is decidedly more affluent than the apartment where he was living when he would take Rita. He bought this new house to erase the memories of Rita sharing his bed in his old apartment. He goes up the stairs from the street and uses his key to open the door to his lavish entry hall. His entire home is carefully and expensively decorated. Daniel has become accustomed to the finer things in life.

He pauses and calls out, "I'm home!"

Shirley, a forty-year-old woman, has been waiting for his return, and she tells him just that. "I've been waiting for you."

Who is Shirley? Has Daniel moved on from Rita? Even though he is still in love with Rita, can he be blamed for finding someone new? Exactly what is the relationship between Daniel and this Shirley? A question soon answered.

Daniel takes out some money and pays her. "Thanks, Shirley."

She takes the money and puts it in her purse. "I'll get the windows done next time."

And then she picks up her cleaning supplies and exits. After she goes, Daniel looks around at his newly cleaned house. His house. He never calls it his home. A home would have a family in it. This is just a well-decorated, well-maintained house. His cleaning lady, Shirley, has done a good job. It's as spotless as it always is when she leaves.

He takes off his coat as he enters his bedroom, which is … as well-appointed as the rest of the house. He hangs up the coat in the closet that is filled with nicely tailored pants, shirts, and coats. On the shelf are shoes that are equally expensive and well-shined. Being a doctor pays well.

He leaves the closet and sits on the bed. Being at Nathan's bar mitzvah has caused him to reflect on how life takes turns that he neither expected nor wanted. On the nightstand is the same picture of Rita and him. He allows the loneliness to creep in.

*

And three more years pass. In the city, the number of cars now far surpasses the number of horses. New York City is the center of civilization, and progress is everywhere—everywhere except at New World Lights and Lamps.

Progress breeds competition. Whereas Mikal had the only lighting store in lower Manhattan, two other stores have taken up residence there. And Mikal has trouble competing since both of the other stores make their own products in their own workspaces and have lower prices. Even though Mikal provides more personal service, his sales have dropped precipitously.

It's a fateful Monday. Before, Mondays had always been the busiest day of the week, but not anymore. There are only two customers, and both are buying lightbulbs from Willum. Mikal's profits depend on people buying fixtures, and because of decreased profits, he has had to let both Moshe and Anthony go. It pained him as first he moved them to part-time, and then he had to let them go permanently. This decision ate at the goodhearted Mikal, but he was glad that both of them found work elsewhere—even though that work was at Mikal's competitors.

Jerome is looking out the main door and scouting for customers. Mikal joins Jerome on the sidewalk. He tells Jerome, "If you look for customers, they never come."

Mikal comes back inside just as the two customers leave with their small purchases. He and Jerome commiserate. A minute later, Mikal tells Willum, "I don't know what we're going to do."

"Maybe business will get better."

Mikal shakes his head. "Neither one of us believes that."

They look out at Jerome, who is still outside the store. Willum know what Mikal is thinking and says, "But Jerome is a good worker."

Mikal says, "When there's work, he's a good worker. I can't pay for a good worker and a manager."

Willum knows what that means for Jerome. "Can we wait until after the holidays?"

"Of course."

*

Daniel's house is a few miles from where Rita and Mikal live. Carrying his doctor's bag, Daniel leaves his brownstone and hails a cab. Cabs are starting to be more present in New York, and they account for lots of the traffic. Their distinctive red and green colors distinguish them from other cars on the road. Daniel hails one, which pulls over to let him in. After Daniel settles in the backseat, the driver reasonably and accurately assumes from the black bag Daniel carries that this passenger must be a doctor. "Where to, Doctor?"

"Third Avenue and Fortieth."

The driver turns and starts to go the fastest way. Daniel stops him. "But can you go down Sixth?"

"I can go anywhere you want, but it's out of the way. It will cost you more."

"I know."

The driver shrugs and makes the turn. They drive silently for a while. The cab driver feels obligated to make conversation. "So you work at the hospital?"

'Yes, I do."

"Do you cut people open?"

"When I have to."

"I don't know that I could do that."

"I guess we're even. I don't know that I could drive a cab."

Daniel doesn't want to talk anymore. He watches the buildings go by until the cab passes Rita and Mikal's building. Daniel says to the cabbie, "Can you slow down?"

"That will cost you more too."

"I know."

The cabbie slows.

Daniel says, "Even slower."

"Okay."

The cabbie slows to a speed where he is barely moving at all.

Daniel looks up toward Mikal and Rita's apartment. Through the window, he can clearly see Rita, Mikal, and Nathan. Nathan has grown into a sixteen-year-old. They are having dinner with Willum in the dining room. Daniel was hoping to catch a glimpse of them, and he has.

Satisfied, he turns to the cabbie. "We can go now."

The cabbie says, "How fast?"

"Fast." And they drive off.

*

The dinner with Willum is not a happy one. Though Willum is almost like family, and Willum has had dinner at their home many times, this time there is a pall over this meal. Everyone is tentative, as if a difficult subject has yet to be brought up. They have finished dessert. Mikal is the first to continue to avoid the issue. "Rita, that was delicious."

Then Rita avoids with a quick, "Thank you."

Then Willum follows suit. "Yes. Best meal for me this week."

Rita gets up and starts clearing dishes. She doesn't want to be there for whatever Mikal has to say to Willum. She leaves the men to talk. Mikal doesn't want Nathan to hear it either. "Nathan, will you help your mother with the dishes? Mr. Van Hoff and I have to talk."

Nathan is a bright young man. He senses the mood. "Sure, Poppa." And he leaves to join his mother in the kitchen.

Mikal and Willum stand. Mikal leads Willum into the living room. Mikal sits in the easy chair facing the couch where Willum sits. Willum tries to make light of the situation, "This must be serious. I never sit here." Then Willum goes on. "Mikal, we've known each other a long time. Can I make it easy on you?"

Mikal is surprised. He thought he'd be the one to bring up the subject. "You don't know what I'm going to say."

A box of cigars rests on an end table. Willum indicates, "Mind if I have a cigar?"

"Go ahead."

Willum lights the cigar and continues, "I know why you invited me to dinner. I see how the business is going. We've already let everyone else go. Even Jerome. It's my turn. I understand that."

Mikal has always appreciated Willum's intelligence as well as his direct attitude. He tells Willum, "Willum, you're a very nice man. If there were any way I could make it work, I would."

Willum puffs on the cigar. "You've made it work for me for a long time. You've kept me on for a year while you were losing money."

Mikal says, "Stay until you find another job."

Willum smiles. "I already found another job. One step ahead. That's what you taught me to be."

Mikal wonders if what Willum is saying is true. Does Willum really have another job? Or is he trying to leave Mikal's store with dignity for both Willum and for himself? Mikal feels obligated to take Willum at his word. "You know something? You're a good friend." With that, Mikal also takes a cigar and lights it. The difficulty of the conversation is over.

Rita smells the cigar smoke and knows that the mood has changed. She calls into the living room, "Can I bring you some coffee?"

Mikal calls back, "Sure. Why not? I'll have coffee with my friend."

Then Willum says to Mikal, "Between you and me, that's much better than having coffee with my boss."

*

As Daniel is used to doing, he continues to stop by the delicatessen to see Hyman and Rose. Over the years, Hyman has expanded his business, and the deli has grown into a restaurant with tables and then more tables. On this Tuesday, after working at the hospital, Daniel comes by. Before he enters, he sees that Hyman isn't behind the counter. Hyman is supervising both the counter and the restaurant. At the cash register is Rose, who loves chatting with the customers.

Behind the counter is a worker Daniel hadn't seen before. The man behind the counter is Jerome—the same Jerome who had worked at New World Lights and Lamps. When Daniel followed Mikal into his store, Jerome had not yet started working there, so he had never seen Jerome before.

Now Daniel, though he doesn't know it, is responsible for Jerome getting this new job. When Daniel and Rita would be together, Daniel would tell her about how kind Hyman and Rose were and how they had taken him in and given him a job. And how hard working they are. When Mikal told Rita that he had to let Jerome go, she went to Jerome and told him that Greenbaum's Deli might need somebody. Rita hoped that Hyman and Rose would be touched by Jerome and his disability and would give him a job. She even made sure that Mikal would give Jerome a good recommendation.

Her plan worked when Jerome met with Hyman and Rose. Their hearts were touched, and they offered Jerome a job after he showed Hyman he could use the slicer with only one hand. This is yet another way that Rita and Daniel are in each other's lives without being in each other's lives.

Daniel enters and calls out, "Hello, friends!" and as usual, all business comes to a halt.

Rose sees him and calls out, "Hyman, put out the closed sign!"

Hyman knows what that means. It means Daniel is there. Hyman sees Daniel and puts out the sign simultaneously as Rose calls to the customers. "Finish up. We're closing."

IT MIGHT HAVE BEEN | 137

Jerome pauses at the slicer and wonders what is going on. Rose briefly explains on her way to sitting down with Daniel, "We told you about Dr. Stabinski. He used to work here. Come meet our Daniel."

When the customers leave, and they all sit together with Jerome hovering, Daniel admires how the deli has grown. "Business is good. More tables."

Rose gushes, "More customers; more tables." Then Rose feels the fabric of Daniel's coat. "Harris Tweed. The doctor business must be good for you too."

They muse about their successes and conclude that America is a good place.

Daniel, ever the professional, says, "Your food is delicious, but I must tell you that it may not be the healthiest."

"Always a doctor."

"I guess I can't help it."

Hyman says, "And some of our food—like our chicken soup—is very healthy. It cures colds."

Rose adds, "See? It evens out."

They spend the next hour telling each other fond memories they have shared together. Every once in a while, Jerome would chirp in after a Daniel comment and tells him, "Memories are different for everyone."

Rose accepts that, but she sums it up. "The best thing about memories: They never happened the way we remember them."

All of them laugh at her analysis, but Daniel can't help but think about Rita and wonder if Rita remembers things the way he does.

*

After saying good night to Nathan, Rita enters the bedroom, where she normally would find Mikal under the covers. But these are not normal times for the couple. She finds him lying on the bed on top of the blanket. He is clearly troubled. She knows him well enough not to say anything. She waits for him to speak first. After a difficult silence, Mikal says what is on his mind. "As soon as business turns around, we can hire Willum back."

Rita is surprised. "You said he told you he already had another job."

Mikal gets up and paces. He is worried about business. He answers Rita, "I know people. He said that only to make it easier for me."

"He's a good man."

A long pause. She knows how proud Mikal is, and she rarely intercedes where his business is concerned, but times are different now. They have never faced this kind of economic crisis. Whereas some businesses are doing well, not so New World Lights and Lamps. She decides that if she doesn't say something right now, she may never find the courage. "Mikal, I've been thinking. With Nathan in school until three every day, I can help out in the mornings."

So far, Mikal has not responded, so she continues. "Then, after school, Nathan can come in and be a stock clerk."

Mikal snaps at her, "I won't have that."

She knows that the subject is delicate for him, so she approaches it differently. "I know about lights. I've been listening to talk about lights for years."

The idea challenges Mikal's view of himself. "No."

"You have taken care of us so well. Give the family the chance to help. Don't be stubborn."

He looks at her with love, and he can see how determined she is to help. Reluctantly, he gives in. "But it will only be until things turn around."

She has won him over for now. Who knows what will happen later? Rita says, "Right. Just until then."

He kisses her, grateful that she is there for him.

CHAPTER TWENTY-TWO

It was bound to happen. There was bound to be a moment when somebody from Daniel's world would come into somebody from Rita's world or the other way around. It's not coincidence; it's inevitable. And it happens in the hospital reception area. Rita's friend Ruth enters and crosses directly to the desk where a different receptionist, Sarah, sits where Agnes had been sitting. Ruth isn't in a hurry, so it's obvious to Sarah that Ruth is neither in need of medical help nor here to visit a patient.

Sarah looks up and asks Ruth, "May I help you?"

The effervescent Ruth responds, "Actually, I'd like to help you."

Not what Sarah usually hears. "I don't understand."

Because Rita is helping Mikal at his store, Ruth has afternoons to spare, afternoons she used to spend with Rita. Why not do something useful? She tells Sarah, "I have a teenage son who is in school much of the day, and I'd like to volunteer to help out in the hospital. I can answer phones or work in the gift shop—anything."

Sarah likes Ruth immediately, but who doesn't? "That's very nice of you. Our chief resident, Dr. Stabinski, is always grateful for anyone who wants to help us here."

What? "Dr. Stabinski?" Rita's Dr. Stabinski? How many Dr. Stabinskis can there be? She doesn't know what to do, possibly being this close to the man Rita had talked about, the man Rita still loves. All she can do is say to Sarah, "Dr. Stabinski? Dr. Daniel Stabinski?"

"That's the one."

Should Rita continue asking questions? What should she do? Part of her wants to leave the hospital right now and talk to Rita. Part of her wants to learn more about this Dr. Stabinski.

Sarah, and almost everyone else at the hospital, knows and likes Daniel. She tells Ruth, "Yes, Dr. Stabinski is one of the most prominent doctors in the entire city. We're lucky he is at our hospital. So, you have heard of him?"

Ruth answers, "As a matter of fact, I have."

Back to business. Sarah remembers why Ruth came in—even if Ruth doesn't. She hands Ruth some papers. "Here are some forms to fill out. When you start here, make sure you introduce yourself to Dr. Stabinski. He likes to meet all the volunteers to thank them personally. That's how he is."

"I'll do just that. You've been very helpful. Thank you." Ruth takes the forms and exits.

*

While Rita has been working at New World Lights and Lamps, Ruth has been making herself useful at the hospital. She has really found a purpose. Her cheery disposition makes her one of the most well-liked volunteers.

One afternoon, she passes a patient's room on the second floor. From inside room 242, she hears the patient say, "Three days, and I'll be able to go home? Thank you, Dr. Stabinski."

Dr. Stabinski? Daniel Stabinski is just inside that room! Ruth stops what she's doing and waits in the hallway. This is her chance to actually meet the man with whom her best friend has been involved. She just wants to talk to him when he leaves that patient. No. Too early. Instead, she sees a ward nurse down the hall at the nurse's station. Leaving her cart, Ruth moves there quickly. Ruth says to the nurse, "Dr. Stabinski is in room 242?"

The ward nurse checks a chart. "Yes, that's where he is."

"What else do you know about him?"

That's an odd question from a hospital volunteer. The nurse decides to answer evasively. "What do I need to know? I'm a nurse; he's a doctor."

Ruth won't be dissuaded from learning more. "I was just wondering if he is married."

Now it's getting strange. "Why would you want to know a thing like that?"

Ruth must think fast and invents a plausible reason. "They asked me to organize a party for the staff and their wives and husbands. That's why I need to know. I want to know how to address the invitations."

The ward nurse is relieved and believes Ruth's invented reason for asking. "I don't know if he's married or not. I have not seen a ring. But I will tell you this much: If he is a single man, just about every woman in the hospital would love to be the one to change that—including yours truly."

"Thank you. You've been a real help."

With a bit of a jaunt in her step, Ruth leaves the nurse's station and "accidentally" runs into Daniel, who is just coming out of another patient's room. Ruth sees exactly how handsome Daniel is and understands why Rita is attracted to him. She takes a breath when she intercepts him and asks, "Dr. Stabinski?"

Always available for volunteers, he says, "Yes, I'm Dr. Stabinski."

Ruth is in it now. "My name is Ruth Messirow."

Indeed, Daniel makes it a point to meet all the volunteers. "Are you a new volunteer?"

"Yes."

Daniel tells her, "I don't need to tell you that you provide a real service. Without you volunteers helping, the hospital would fall apart."

Now Ruth expands on the lie that she had told the ward nurse. "And to show our appreciation for you and your staff, the hospital asked me to arrange a small party for all the doctors and nurses and their husbands and wives. I want to make sure to address the envelopes correctly. So there is no Mrs. Stabinski?" This is what Ruth is desperate to know for sure.

Probably thinking about Rita, he says, "No. Just me."

Now Ruth, having gleaned what she was dying to find out, wants to get away from Daniel as fast as she can. "I have to get these flowers to all the patients before they die." Then she realizes what she said. "I mean the flowers, not the patients."

With a laugh, Daniel says, "I know what you meant."

Daniel calls after her as she goes down the hall, "Nice to meet you, Ruth."

*

Ruth, still wearing her hospital clothes, enters New World Lights and Lamps. She is looking for Rita. She spots her friend behind the counter in the nearly empty store. She rushes to Rita immediately.

Rita is surprised to see Ruth in the store. She never comes to New World Lights and Lamps. "Hi, Ruth. What are you doing here?"

Ruth does a quick look around the store before she whispers, "Is Mikal here?"

Ruth has no idea why Ruth is acting so conspiratorially. "No. He went to the bank. He goes every day at this time to deposit the receipts."

"I know."

That Ruth knows is proof that Ruth doesn't want Mikal around to hear what she has to say.

Rita says, "What are you trying not to tell me?"

Ruth tries to find the words to open the subject. She decides to ease in. "You know I volunteer at the hospital."

Rita now suspects where this is going. "Yes, I know that."

Ruth sees in her friend's face that she is ahead of what Ruth has to say. Ruth tells Rita, "I saw him."

Maybe she isn't necessarily talking about Daniel, but Rita knows that's exactly who's she's talking about. She asks pointlessly, "Who?"

"Your Dr. Stabinski."

"Oh, no."

"Oh, yes."

If Rita could stop Ruth from continuing, she would, but then again, she wants to know what Ruth is about to tell her. Ruth is intent on getting Rita to hear it all. "And I found out he's not married, and I don't know if you know—but he's rich."

These are things Rita would want to know, but Rita wants to know something first. "Is he well?"

"Well and handsome."

Rita is both upset and curious. "Why were you snooping?"

Ruth is defensive. "I wasn't. It was an accident. Absolutely unintentional. I just thought you'd be interested."

Rita comes out from behind the counter. Rita tells Ruth, "Ruth, stay out of this."

Ruth's feelings are hurt. "I was just trying to help."

"Help what?"

"You and Daniel."

Rita moves even further away from Ruth. "There is no me and Daniel. I don't care." Then Rita speaks mostly to herself. "I can't care."

Ruth now goes directly to her distraught friend. "But you said—"

"I know what I said. You know Mikal?"

"Of course."

"And you like him?"

"You know that I do. He's a wonderful man."

"Then don't make this more complicated than it already is."

"I just thought—"

"Don't think anymore. Please. Be a good friend and don't do anymore."

As Ruth ponders whether or not she should have told Rita what she told her, she says, "Okay. Have it your way."

Starting to leave, Ruth runs into Mikal, who is returning from the bank. "Hi, Ruth. It's so nice to see you."

Ruth answers, "Yeah? Well, tell that to your wife."

Mikal assumes there must have been some spat between Ruth and his wife when he crosses to Rita. "What was that about?"

Rita tries to dismiss it with, "You know how Ruth gets." Rita decides to change the subject. "What did the bank say?"

Mikal wishes he had better news. When business was booming, he'd come back from the bank, and it would be a celebration since their account was increasing every time he went.

Mikal confesses, "I didn't have much to deposit, and then they told me that they have extended our loan as far as they could. Oh, Rita, it hasn't been a good day for us."

Rita has more than one reason to agree, "No, it hasn't."

*

Delmonico's is the most expensive and fanciest restaurant in New York City. Everyone is dressed in his or her finest: the maître d', the diners, the waiters, the busboys, everyone. Daniel is already seated at a table where he sips from a glass of wine while he waits for his dinner companions.

Pat and Laurie come into the restaurant and are immediately wide-eyed. They have never eaten in a restaurant as fashionable as this, and everything about it amazes them. They move to the maître d's stand.

Pat says, "We're looking for Daniel Stabinski."

Of course, Henry, the maître d', knows Daniel since Daniel eats there often. "Dr. Stabinski is at his usual table. Right this way."

As Pat and Laurie follow Henry to Daniel's table, they continue to be impressed by the opulence of the restaurant. They reach Daniel, and he stands to greet them. He shakes hands with Pat and kisses Laurie's cheek and says, "It's been too long."

Pat can't help himself from asking, "Do you eat here a lot?"

"When I can." He adds, "Let's get this decided right away. This dinner is on me. When I come out your way, it'll be on you."

Thank God, Daniel is generous. No way could they afford to pay whatever the dinner might cost. Now they sit, and Pat says to Laurie. "Didn't I tell you about him? He eats here a lot. Look at this place. Hoby and I always knew he'd make it big."

Daniel has an attempt at modesty. "But I work long hours. I'm hardly ever home to cook."

Laurie then assumes, "And you never got married?"

"I never found the right person, somebody who would put up with my crazy schedule."

Pat reaches into his pocket and pulls out pictures. He shows them to the interested Daniel. "These are what happens when you get married."

Laurie points them out proudly. "The big guy is Pat Junior, the eight-year-old is Mary Ellen, and the young one is Brian. We gave him the middle name 'Hoby.'"

Pat says, "Hoby should not be forgotten."

That touches Daniel, who says, "You're a mensch."

Laurie and Pat look at each other. "Mensch?"

Daniel explains, "A mensch is a person, or in your case, people, who do good things when they don't have to."

Their conversation is interrupted by a waiter who hands out menus. "Do you want to hear our specials?"

Pat has to comment, "We never ate in a restaurant that had specials before."

The rest of the meal is spent catching up. Before they came to the restaurant, both Pat and Laurie were afraid that Daniel might have changed, but other than becoming wealthy, Daniel is still the warm, generous man they knew years ago. If they knew how to pronounce "mensch" correctly, Pat and Laurie would conclude that Daniel is indeed a mensch.

*

Since Nathan is in school until the afternoon, Rita is free to help Mikal at the store. It takes pressure from Mikal in one way, but it adds emotional pressure. Mikal feels that he has somehow failed the family. Rita does what she can to dissuade him from that belief, but he can't help feeling what he feels. Mikal loves Nathan, and he loves seeing him in the afternoon at New World Lights and Lamps, but Nathan's very presence there is another reminder of how the business is failing.

Today when Nathan comes in, Rita is at the customer counter, but there are no customers.

He kisses her and greets her, "Hi, Mom."

"How was school today?"

"Have you ever heard of algebra?"

"No."

"I wish I hadn't. Where's Poppa?"

"He's in the back putting away some inventory."

"I'll go help him."

Nathan starts off, but Rita stops him. "Would you do me a favor instead?"

He spins back. "Sure."

"I'm going home to fix dinner. Just watch the store and call out to your poppa if any customers come in."

"Okay."

Rita leaves the store. Nathan waits for a moment, sees that no one is coming into the store, and decides to check in with Mikal. He goes to the storeroom and sees Mikal moving a large crate toward the shelves. The boy goes to help. "Hi, Poppa."

Mikal is grateful for any possible help. "Nathan, can you give me a hand?"

Nathan would like to, but he remembers what his mother said. "Mom told me to watch the front of the store in case there are any customers."

Mikal doesn't want Nathan to disobey Rita. "Okay. You do that. I will manage here."

Nathan kisses Mikal and returns to the sales floor. Mikal watches Nathan leave, and then he resumes the task at hand. The crate is extremely heavy. It would be fairly easy to lift if he still had some employees to help, but now it's up to him alone, and he's not as young as he used to be. He pushes at the crate and manages to get it closer to the shelves. He bends at the knees to pick it up, and, after straining, is able to do that. Now it's just an inch or two short of making it to the shelf, but it's no use. He pauses to catch his breath. Then he tries even harder and accidentally knocks the shelf unit, causing a large (and even heavier crate) to fall from the top shelf and crash onto a heavy box on the next shelf. It's a domino effect that causes them to land as a unit on Mikal, who is pinned below!

In the main store, Nathan is jolted when he hears the loud crashing sound and Mikal's anguished scream.

Nathan yells out, "Poppa!" No answer. He yells "Poppa!" again as he runs.

Nathan enters the storeroom. When he comes in, his worst fears are realized. At first, he can't see Mikal since he is buried under the crates. Then Nathan finally sees Mikal wedged beneath the extremely heavy crates. Mikal moans in agony. Nathan moves some lighter boxes out of the way and braces his back against the larger crate and pushes with all his might, but it won't budge. All the while, he calls, "Poppa! Poppa, are you all right, right? Talk to me!"

Mikal is barely audible. "Nathan, Nathan, I can't move. And I'm hurt … very bad." This inspires Nathan to try even harder to get the crate off Mikal, but it's no use. "I can't move it!"

The frustrated and desperate Nathan is at a loss as to how to help. "Poppa, what should I do?"

Mikal realizes the hopelessness of his situation and comes to a fateful decision. "Go to the hospital. Ask for Dr. Stabinski. Go now!"

Nathan, anxious to help in any way, says, "I'm going right now!"

He runs out of the storeroom, out of the empty store, and out the door.

Mikal tries to get air, but more and more breath is hard to find. Fearing the worst, Mikal knows exactly why he specifically wanted Daniel to come.

Nathan runs down the block, past stores and people. He jostles some as he runs, and some think the teenage boy is rude, but Nathan doesn't care what anybody thinks. He must do what he can to save his poppa as he runs faster than he ever has in his life. Mikal's very life is at stake. Nathan makes it to the hospital and runs up to the reception desk. A lady in front of him is questioning Sarah about what street has a bus running at this hour.

Nathan would normally wait, but he can't. He gets out a panicked, "Please. My poppa!"

Hearing the boy's desperation, the woman moves out of the way and allows Nathan to take her place in front of Sarah. "Dr. Stabinski—please, I need Dr. Stabinski. My poppa—" Nathan collapses in frightened tears, and Sarah comes out from her desk to help him. As she does, an attendant, Richard, walks by.

She calls to him, "Richard, get Dr. Stabinski. Now!"

Richard sees the emergency unfolding and runs off to find Daniel. Sarah turns to the distraught Nathan. "What's the matter? What has happened?"

Daniel has just come out of surgery and is washing his hands when Richard races in. "Dr. Stabinski, come quick."

"What? What is it?"

"Sarah said, 'Get Dr. Stabinski' like she meant it."

Daniel quickly finishes drying his hands, grabs his medical bag, and follows Richard out, down the halls, and then down the stairs into the reception area where he sees a nurse helping Nathan. Nathan? Daniel can't believe Nathan is in the hospital and asking for him. What is it? Did something happen to him? Did something happen to Rita? Daniel knows that Nathan wouldn't recognize him when he asks, "What is it? What's wrong?"

"My poppa told me to bring you. There's been an accident. At the store."

Daniel doesn't need to hear anymore. "Come. Let's go."

As they move quickly to the door, the nurse calls after them, "Dr. Stabinski, you have the Felber appendix surgery at four o'clock!"

Daniel yells back, "Have Dr. Hilton do it. I'll be back when I can."

Now they're on the street. Fortunately, there are always cabs near the hospital entrance. Daniel opens the rear of the cab and pushes Nathan in.

IT MIGHT HAVE BEEN | 149

This would be a big moment for Nathan, who had never ridden in a cab before, but this is no time to acknowledge it. Too much is at stake. Daniel says to the cabbie, "Eight North Houston Street."

Nathan can't understand why Daniel would know the address. "Dr. Stabinski, you know where my poppa's store is?"

As far as Nathan knows, why would Daniel know? Daniel covers the topic as best as he can. "I know your parents. I even know you."

"You do?"

"Yes. I came to dinner once when you were a small boy. We can talk about that later. Right now, tell me what happened."

"I was in the front of the store working when I heard a loud crash. Poppa yelled out for me. I ran there, and some big crates knocked him to the ground, and he couldn't get out. He can't get out. I pushed and I pushed, and I couldn't move the crates."

"He's still underneath them?"

"Yes. That was when he told me to get you."

"Did you see how badly he is hurt?"

"I couldn't see."

By the time they reach the store, Daniel has taken some dollar bills out of his pocket. Nathan jumps out, and Daniel pays the cabbie and catches up with Nathan in the showroom. Nathan yells out, "Poppa, we're here. I got the doctor!"

They run to the storeroom together and see that Mikal is still trapped. Mikal is decidedly weaker.

Nathan kisses Mikal's brow. "The doctor is here."

Mikal says, "Good. Good."

Daniel immediately starts to assess the situation while telling Mikal, "I'm here, Mikal."

Mikal has barely enough strength to stay, "Thank you for coming."

Nathan was too busy trying to help Mikal to cry. Now he bursts into tears and pleads to Daniel, "Is my poppa going to be okay?"

Daniel feels obligated to tell the truth. "I hope so. But I can't tell yet. Not until we get him out from under there. Help me move these crates." With great effort, Daniel and Nathan work together to budge the crate off Mikal, who calls out in pain.

Daniel tells them, "Sorry."

Daniel and Nathan push more, and Mikal tries his best to quietly bear the pain. Then, with an extreme effort, they move the crate enough to slide Mikal out from underneath. When they do, Daniel quickly examines Mikal and immediately concludes that Mikal's chest has been crushed. Daniel has seen enough trauma in the war to realize Mikal can't survive this. Daniel hides the seriousness from Nathan. Mikal is fading rapidly. This scares Nathan, who begs Daniel, "You have to make my poppa better."

Daniel says to Nathan, "Go get your mother."

Nathan objects. "No. I want to stay here with Poppa."

Daniel repeats more forcefully. "Go get your mother *now!*"

Mikal has enough strength to tell Nathan, "Go now."

Nathan kisses his father once again. "I'll be right back, Poppa." Then he runs out of the storeroom.

Daniel bends down close to Mikal's face. Mikal's pain lets him know how badly he is hurt. Still, Daniel can hope. Mikal says, "Is it that bad?"

Daniel takes Mikal's hand in his, and as gently as possible tells Mikal, "I'm sorry. Your whole chest cavity is compressed. All your ribs are crushed and splintered. I'm afraid they're piercing most of your organs."

Mikal accepts the judgment and only wants to know, "Am I going to die?"

Daniel isn't optimistic, yet what good would it do to tell Mikal there is no hope? The best he can say is, "Nobody can tell something like that for certain."

Mikal can infer from Daniel's tone that his condition is hopeless. Suffering, he is able to ask Daniel in a whisper, "How soon? Can we get to the hospital?"

*

Rita is at the stove when the out-of-breath Nathan runs in.

"Mom, come quick. Poppa is hurt. The doctor is with him." This is no time for questions. She turns off the stove, and they run out.

*

Daniel is making it as comfortable as he can for Mikal, who is fading fast. Somehow, Mikal has found enough strength to say, "Daniel, I have to tell you something."

Daniel wants Mikal to save whatever energy he has. "You don't have to tell me anything."

But he does. Despite the convoluted relationship between Rita and Daniel and Mikal and who Nathan's father really is, Mikal is able to say four words: "Be good to them."

Rita and Nathan rush through the showroom. For this time, it is lucky that there are no customers. Then they run into the storeroom. Rita can't believe the sight in front of her. She is shocked. Not just that her husband is near death, but the doctor who has been tending to him is Daniel. Rita screams, "Oh, my God!"

Filled with every emotion, she goes to Mikal. Daniel stands back. Nathan and his mother kneel over Mikal.

Rita says, "Mikal ..."

Nathan says, "Poppa ..."

Rita turns back to Daniel. "Is he going to be all right?" Daniel says nothing, but she and Nathan can read his face. She collapses into Daniel.

Nathan cries, "No!" And then he beats on Daniel's chest. He's not mad at Daniel, he's mad at God for letting this happen to Mikal. He implores Daniel, "You have to make my poppa well. You have to!"

Mikal whispers to Nathan, "Nathan, come here."

Nathan leaves Daniel and goes to Mikal, who, with great difficulty, says, "Nathan, you have to be good. You have to take care of your mother."

Nathan knows what Mikal is asking, but he won't acknowledge that Mikal will soon be gone. "No, Poppa, you can't die."

Rita now comes close. Mikal's last words as Rita is near his face are, "Rita ... Nathan ... I—" Before he can complete the thought, Mikal takes his last breath.

Nathan screams for both him and his mother. "No, Poppa. No, Poppa. No, Poppa!"

His anguished cries echo as Daniel and Rita collapse into each other. They don't hold each other as lovers. They hold each other as two people sharing the tragedy of what has just happened.

CHAPTER TWENTY-THREE

Mikal's funeral is one of the saddest that the Congregation Rodeph Shalom has ever witnessed. It's one thing when someone old passes away, like Rita's father, but when someone in the center of his life is suddenly gone, the grief is magnified tenfold. Everyone who knew Mikal is there—his family, his friends, those he worked with. He was truly loved.

Daniel is there too. He was there when Mikal died, and nobody would question the propriety of his attendance.

The rabbi says all the appropriate words when he tells the assembled that God decides, and man must accept. That sentiment is rarely believed by the loved ones of the deceased, but the rabbi is compelled to say it.

Rita doesn't believe it. Nathan doesn't believe it. Rita and Nathan rise at the same time to go to the front of the congregation where they will speak together. It is unusual for two people to address the mourners at the same time, but Rita and Nathan lean on each other for support. Among other things, Rita says, "Mikal was a great husband."

Among other things, Nathan says, "Mikal is a great father. Is not 'was' because he is still in my heart, and he will be forever."

The pain of this statement brings everyone to tears.

Rita kisses Nathan and tells him, "Poppa loved you so much."

Rita looks up and catches sight of Daniel. She gives him the slightest nod, a nod that is imperceptible to anyone else.

Earlier, there were other speakers, including Mikal's brothers, Willum, and two of his customers, but nobody will remember anybody other than the grieving Rita and Nathan.

*

Daniel walks down the hall of the patients' rooms. As he does, nurses, interns, and doctors always pepper him with questions and requests, such as: "Who do I see about scheduling?" "What is the protocol for releasing patients?" "Can patients bring their own food into the hospital?"

Some of the questions really should be asked of other people, but Daniel pleasantly answers each one. All in his day's work.

On this day, Daniel heads for one of the larger patient rooms. He knocks and doesn't wait for a response before entering. "Hello."

Hyman is in the bed as Rose sits by his side in a chair. Hyman says to Daniel, "You had to get me such a big room?"

Rose says, "Hyman, our Daniel is a big shot. He can put you in any room he wants."

Daniel gets down to business. He has the test results. "It is just as I suspected. It's gout."

Rose says, "Gout? Oh, no. Gout." And then she adds, "What is this gout?"

Daniel says to Hyman, "The reason you fell is that your feet are a little bloated, and that makes it hard to walk sometimes."

Hyman says, "I have to walk. That's what I do at the deli."

Daniel approaches the subject gingerly. "That's the reason for gout. Some people call gout 'the rich man's disease.' It comes from eating rich food."

Hyman is proud of the appellation. "A rich man's disease."

Rose is more practical, "You want us to sell worse food? How is that going to make my Hyman better?"

Daniel laughs and says to Hyman, "No. I just want you to be more careful about what you yourself eat. Can you do that?"

Hyman says, "And if I don't?"

"I like you, but I'd be seeing you back here. I'd rather see you at the deli."

Hyman and Rose look at each other. It will be a tough order for Hyman, who loves eating his deli food.

Rose finally makes the decision for her husband and says to Daniel, "You're the doctor."

Daniel then says to Hyman, "Then do what the doctor says." Daniel kisses both of them, and when he starts out the door, he tosses back, "You can go home this afternoon."

*

The next weeks are a sad blur for Rita and Nathan. Mikal's brothers and their families huddle around Rita and Nathan to help them through all that must be done when someone dies so unexpectedly. No one had prepared them for this. The funeral, taking care of all the many things that Mikal used to do for them, makes his loss even more profound. And the store. What to do about the store? Though it was less and less profitable, New World Lights and Lamps was the center of Mikal's life. For a while, Rita wouldn't go to the store at all, and it remained fallow. Dust was creeping through the closed windows and door. But how could she return there? The image she had of Mikal dying in that place is far too wrenching a memory for her to revisit.

One day, Josef and Goldie and Sid and Sadie come to Rita. Mikal's brothers bring their wives to help support Rita when they say what they feel must be said.

Josef, now the patriarch of the family, speaks for all of them. "Rita, we know how hard this is for you. And it's hard for all of us. But you have to sell the store. You have to."

"But it was Mikal's life."

Goldie tells her, "You and Nathan were Mikal's life."

And now Sid says, "It is breaking you. He would want you to do what's best. And what's best is selling the store."

Rita looks at all of them. They are only there because they have Rita's and Nathan's best interests at heart.

She whispers, "You're right. It's just so hard."

They hold her close with love.

*

Just because she won't have to bear the weight of keeping New World Lights and Lamps open doesn't make life easier for her. Nathan is in school, and Rita is glad he won't be here to witness the end of Mikal's dream. The store is filled with boxes as the inventory is being emptied for sale. This is bittersweet for Rita. And Mikal would have known what to do.

Willum has shown up to help Rita. He is everywhere at once doing most of the packing and moving. They take a break, which gives Rita a chance to talk to him privately. "You have a job; you didn't have to come back and help with all this."

"Mrs. Glass, your husband treated me very well. It's the least I could do. Besides, you knew Mikal. He'd come out of the grave to kill me if I didn't." Enough said. Willum leaves her to go off to direct a workman as to where to move some of the goods.

It's time-consuming hard work because half the time, Rita looks at a lamp and doesn't want to let it go. It means too much to her. She looks at a fixture and remembers Mikal holding that same fixture. She tries to decide which lot to place it in. That, too, is difficult. Letting it go is letting go of Mikal all over again.

During the painful process, Ruth comes into the store and works her way through the boxes until she arrives at where Rita is standing. They had not seen each other for a couple of weeks. For them, that would be a long time. Ruth sees the nostalgia that is overwhelming her friend and asks her gently, "How are you doing?"

"Ruth, this is so hard."

"I know."

"But finishing here is keeping me busy. I imagine there will be a day when living without Mikal will be easier, but this is not that day.

"You can use a man's help."

"Willum is here."

Then Rita calls out to Willum. "Willum, look who's here. It's Mrs. Messirow!"

Willum stops working long enough to wave hello and then returns to what he was doing.

Ruth was not talking about a man to help in the store. She continues her original thought. "On the way here, I walked past the hospital."

Rita is not prepared for this discussion—not yet, if ever. "Don't start, Ruth."

"Why not? It's been three months. Has he called?"

"No."

"Then he's waiting for you to call him. He was at Mikal's funeral. I saw him there."

Rita says, "You didn't say anything, did you?"

"What would I say? The women in the neighborhood think—"

Rita pulls Ruth away from the workmen. She doesn't want them to hear what she and Ruth are talking about, especially since Rita doesn't want to talk about it.

"I don't care what the women in the neighborhood think."

Ruth won't let it go. "Let me finish. They don't know anything about you and Dr. Stabinski from before. They just see an available doctor and an attractive widow and think you can make each other happy."

"Ruth, stop."

Ruth won't. "Rita, you told me that you think Dr. Stabinski could even be Nathan's real father."

Rita snaps back at her, "If you ever said anything about that—"

"I didn't. I promised I wouldn't. What kind of a friend do you think I am?"

Rita says, "I'm starting to wonder."

Ruth pushes, "But if that's true or even if it isn't, don't you think Nathan would be better off having a father in his life?"

Rita says, "I can't call Daniel. I won't."

Ruth is frustrated by her friend's stubbornness. "That's your last word on that?"

"Yes. And I want it to be your last word on it too."

Any more discussion is interrupted when Willum comes over to them. "Everything is just about ready for the trucks."

Rita says to him, "I can never thank you enough, Willum."

The modest Willum says, "Well, then stop trying."

Willum goes off to finalize what needs to be done. Rita and Ruth look around as the store is being emptied. Rita tells Ruth, "It'll be strange seeing another store in here."

"What kind of a store is taking over?"

"They sell radios."

"Radios? Who'd buy their own radio when you can just listen to somebody else's?"

CHAPTER TWENTY-FOUR

Rita has done little to change the apartment that she, Mikal, and Nathan shared. In some ways it's as if Mikal were still there. His spirit is definitely there tonight when Rita and Nathan are at the kitchen table where they look at literature about different colleges. It's hard to believe, but Nathan is leaving high school and getting ready to take the next step. They have separated the written material from the schools he is considering; ones he is considering seriously; and ones he has no interest in.

Nathan asks Rita, "Do you want to go over them again with me?"

Rita says, "We've already been over them and over them again. If you have to choose one right now, which college?"

"I would pick the one Poppa would have wanted."

"And that would be?"

He holds up some literature from New York University. "Poppa would want me to go to a college nearby, so I could take care of you."

Rita kisses her son affectionately. "You don't have to 'take care of me.' Stop worrying about me. Your poppa would be happy anywhere you'd go. Our son is going to college. That would make him so proud."

He hugs her back, and this moment is broken up when the telephone rings. They're happy they no longer must share a party line with Mr. Weisborg.

Nathan answers. "Hello. Yes, Dr. Stabinski ... we're doing a little better, thanks. She's right here."

Rita freezes. She has overheard that Daniel is on the phone. She takes a breath to compose herself.

Nathan puts his hand over the phone and whispers to Rita, "It's Dr. Stabinski."

She takes the phone from Nathan, who returns to examining the college literature. Since Nathan is right next to her, Rita is careful as to what she says. "Hello, Dr. Stabinski."

Daniel is in his office at the hospital, and the conversation is awkward for him as well. He doesn't quite know what to say either. "Hello. Is this a bad time?"

"No."

Daniel says, "I was hoping you'd call, but a little bird of a volunteer at the hospital 'volunteered' that you weren't going to."

Rita knows who that volunteer is. "Ruth?"

"Don't tell her I told you."

Rita looks at Nathan. She decides to obfuscate the nature of the call. When she does, Daniel catches on.

"Dr. Stabinski, I don't know if—"

To make sure, he says, "Is Nathan nearby?"

Rita says, "That's exactly it, Dr. Stabinski."

"But we can talk later?"

"That's right. Thank you for calling."

They both hang up. Daniel smiles. He knows that they had a past, and now he knows that they can have a future.

Nathan asks Rita, "What did the doctor want?"

"He's a good man. And he's a good doctor. He wanted to know if we were doing okay."

That satisfies Nathan, and Rita is glad that it does.

*

Daniel is coming home from work. As he gets through the front door, the phone is ringing. He tosses his medical bag on the entry table and picks up the phone.

Rita is alone in her apartment. "It's me."

Daniel is thrilled. "Oh, hi. I'm so glad you called."

"Nathan isn't home, and I didn't want you to guess when to call."

A pause. And then Daniel says, "I love you. You know that."

It comes easily and not hard for her to say, "And I love you."

That's all that needs to be said in this conversation.

*

It's as if they were young lovers and trying to make up for lost time. The first place they visit together is the dock in lower Manhattan. Not only is this where both Rita and Daniel first landed in America, this is also where the troop ship arrived when Daniel came back from the war. It has a special dual meaning. They look out at the Statue of Liberty. In a way, they feel they are finally given the liberty to be together.

Daniel takes Rita to Delmonico's. The maître d' welcomes him. "Good to see you again, Dr. Stabinski."

The waiters and maître d' know him well, but this is the first time they have seen him bring a female companion. Daniel introduces Rita. "Henry, this is Rita. You'll be seeing her often."

"Very nice to meet you, Henry."

"Nice to meet you, Rita."

Henry turns to Daniel. "Your usual table?"

"No. This time it's different. Let Rita decide."

Rita and Daniel have been in the shadows for too long. She feels emboldened enough to say, "Someplace where people can see us."

Henry says, "Right this way."

Daniel smiles. He enjoys seeing Rita blossom this way. They pass Daniel's old table, and Henry takes them to a table in the center of the restaurant. "Will this table be all right?"

They both say "perfect" at the same time. Then they laugh. They have that kind of communication.

*

It's the end of the week. The doctors, nurses, and staff of the hospital normally would be heading to their homes. Not this day. All are with their husbands and wives and move to the all-purpose room of the hospital, though they don't know what today's purpose is. Sarah asks one of the nurses, "Why are we staying after work? And why are these other people here?"

The nurse says, "Dr. Stabinski says he wants us here, and when the chief resident says we should go, we go."

The all-purpose room is decorated for a party. Daniel and Rita are at the front of the room, where they wait for everyone to gather. No one is more surprised to see Rita there than Ruth and her husband, Aaron. Daniel speaks to everyone. "A while ago, one of our volunteers pretended to throw a party for everyone at the hospital. There was never going to be a party. Why would Ruth Messirow do that?"

All eyes turn to Ruth, who has a mea culpa look.

Daniel continues, "She did this for the sole purpose of finding out if I had a wife or a close female friend. Shame on you, Ruth. However, since that time, I have found—or re-found—someone close, and I'd like you all to meet her. This is Rita."

Everyone is shocked. Dr. Stabinski has always been one who keeps his personal life to himself. They all greet Rita warmly.

He goes on. "In order to make Ruth's party a real one, we thought we'd throw this party. And Ruth, as you can see, I now have someone in my life. Everyone, enjoy the food and drink."

A good time is had by all. Daniel takes Rita's hand, and they move to be next to Ruth and Aaron. Aaron says to Daniel, "Dr. Stabinski, it's nice to finally meet you. Between you and me, I tell her not to butt in, but she doesn't listen."

Daniel tells Aaron, "What's done is done."

Rita elbows Daniel. "You could have said, 'I'm glad she did.'"

Daniel kids Ruth, "I don't want to give her too much credit."

The four laugh.

Then Daniel says, "Rita and I want to know if you'd like to go out together, maybe go to a play with us."

Ruth quickly answers for both her and Aaron. "We'd love to."

*

Daniel and Rita and Ruth and Aaron are dressed in their finest as they move down the sidewalk on Second Avenue on the lower East Side. They are on their way to the theatre and pass several Yiddish playhouses. Ruth says to Rita, "When you asked us if we wanted to see a play, we thought you meant a Broadway play."

They reach their destination. It's the Yiddish Arts Theatre, where the signage indicates the title: *Der Dibek* (*The Dybbuk*), also known by its original title, *Tsvishn Tsvey Veltn* (*Between Two Worlds*).

Rita is the most excited. "Come in. You'll love it."

Aaron is not so sure as they walk to the ticket window where Daniel steps up and, in Yiddish, asks for four tickets: *"Fir bite."*

He takes the tickets. They go through the lobby where he hands them to the usher, and they proceed inside. As they watch the play performed in Yiddish, Rita is completely enthralled with the acting and the story, as is Daniel.

Ruth and Aaron have not been to a play before—of any kind. Ruth is equally mesmerized, but Aaron doesn't seem interested at all.

The stage is set with two graves upstage. Downstage is a wedding party. At a particularly dramatic moment where guests are gathered for the wedding, in the audience Rita is moved to tears while on the stage are Leah, Hahman, Menashe, Reb Mendl. Leah is the young woman who has been forced to marry. Menashe is her betrothed and is in the process of putting a wedding veil on her head—a veil she does not want. Sender is Leah's father, who wants her to marry. It's a mystical play with evil spirits at work.

Leah tears off the veil and cries to Menashe as she pushes him away. *"You are not my bridegroom!"*

Great confusion among all those on stage as they surround Leah.

Sender is shaking and yells at Leah, *"My daughter, my daughter! What is it?"*

Leah tears herself away and runs to the grave, spreads her arms, and yells, *"Holy bride and groom, protect me! Save me!"*

She falls; people run to her and lift her up; she looks around wild-eyed and cries out—but not with her own voice but with that of a man who has possessed her. *"Ah! Ah! You have buried me! But I have returned to my promised bride and will not leave her!"*

Nahman, Menashe's father, is shaking and screams, *"She is mad!"*

The Messenger, a sinister unnamed traveler, declares, *"A dybbuk has entered the body of the bride."*

With this declaration, the curtain falls to end the act. The audience applauds.

Caught up in the sentiment of the play, Rita and Ruth clap through tears. Daniel applauds as well, but he is mostly supportive of Rita's emotions. Aaron applauds but with less vigor.

Outside the theatre after the performance, the crowd pours into the street. Rita and Ruth are still recovering from the excitement of the play. As they walk away, Daniel notices that Aaron is subdued. Daniel says, "You didn't like the play?"

Aaron says loud enough so that Rita and Ruth hear him, "I didn't want to say anything since you all liked it so much, but I don't speak Yiddish."

Hearing that, all of them, including Aaron, break into laughter. Still laughing, they walk away from Second Avenue.

*

Aaron and Ruth are in bed in their apartment. Ruth comments, "Wasn't that a great evening?"

"Except for me not understanding a word of the play."

Ruth asks, "What do you think of Daniel?"

Aaron says, "I liked Mikal. I really did. But there's something natural about the way Rita is with Daniel. It's good to see her smiling again."

Rita says, "You are so right."

Aaron asks, "How long did you say they know each other?"

"I didn't say."

Aaron says, "It just seems like they belong together."

Ruth could say so much more; but for this one time, she doesn't. Instead, she kisses her husband, turns off the light, rolls over, and goes to sleep with a smile on her face.

*

Daniel had never brought Rita to his new place. Though it is well-appointed, it is decorated for a bachelor. When he opens the door and they go inside, he hopes she'll like it. She doesn't say a word. She is stunned at how opulent it is and says nothing.

He mistakes that silence for not liking it and says so. "You don't like it."

"It's not that. The last time we were together was in your small apartment. That is where I always picture you."

"Do you want to look around?"

"Absolutely."

The foyer leads to the living room. Among the art on the wall are plaques and commendations.

She is impressed. "You were valedictorian at your college? You never told me."

"It didn't come up."

She sees another diploma. "And this one says you were number one in your medical school too? You never told me that either."

"There was a lot I didn't tell you."

She kisses him tenderly. "I want to hear it all, everything I missed."

Kidding her, he says, "Let me see. I always wanted to be a doctor. You knew that."

She kisses him and playfully points to a room she assumes is the bedroom. "Tell me about that room."

Daniel says, "That's my bedroom. That's where I dream about you."

She moves flirtatiously to the bedroom door. "Let's finish the tour later—and make your dreams come true now."

With that, she steps inside. Daniel had his cleaning lady, Shirley, make the room spotless since he anticipated bringing Rita back here with him. Though they are destined to be in the bed, she takes the time to look around the room. It's immaculate. She sees the long-traveled picture of herself and Daniel on the nightstand. She loves seeing it there. She looks at him, opens her arms to him. They kiss. It gets passionate almost immediately.

Daniel stops abruptly. "Wait. I bought you something." He darts into his closet and brings out a sexy nightgown.

She looks at it and says, "Why? I'm not going to be wearing it."

Enough said. She tosses the nightgown on a lounge chair. Clothes come off sensually, and they topple onto the bed. Before they begin to make love, she takes the time to take the picture on the nightstand and turn it away from them. She tells him, "I don't want the competition."

Daniel laughs and kisses her. "What's past is just a path to our future together."

"That's beautiful."

He tells her with complete honesty. "No. You're beautiful."

Their lovemaking is so incredibly right. So passionate. So filled with love. Afterward, they laze in each other's arms.

She reaches for the photograph and speaks to it. "Pretty good, don't you think?"

She and Daniel laugh. She starts to get out of bed. He kiddingly says, "Don't tell me you're leaving."

She doesn't answer him immediately. Instead, she puts on the nightgown he bought for her. Then she says, "No. I don't have to get home. Nathan is at college." She adds, "I'm going into your kitchen, and I'm going to cook for you. That's something I have wanted to do for so many years."

He laughs and says, "Very nice, but you won't find any food in the kitchen. I'm an unmarried man. My icebox echoes."

She comes back to him. "Then what'll we do?"

With sex on his mind, he says, "Come back to bed. Let's see if we can make up for lost time."

Not having to be convinced, she leaps onto him. They laugh and roll over on top of one another.

*

Daniel, Rita, Rose, Pat, Laurie, and Norma are at a table in the deli. There's an empty chair. It's an important event for Daniel, who wants everyone to get to know Rita. Daniel begins by saying, "I want to thank you all for being here."

He is interrupted by Rose. "Daniel, shush. Wait till Hyman comes."

They look over and see Hyman escorting a man and his wife to the cash register where Jerome is working. "Jerome, take care of Mr. and Mrs. Feldstein."

Then Hyman joins the table and sits and says, "Look at me. Sitting in my own restaurant."

Daniel says, "That's okay. It's my party."

Rose turns to Hyman. "Tell him what we decided."

Hyman tells Daniel and the group, "I'm paying. No arguments."

Daniel says reluctantly, "All right."

Hyman adds, "And you can have anything you want. Me? Don't mind me. I'm having soup and cabbage." He winks at Daniel. "Doctor's orders."

Gentile Pat looks at the menu and asks, "What's kishka?"

Rose looks at Pat, assumes correctly that he's not Jewish, and tells him, "If you have to ask what it is, you won't like it."

Pat accepts the advice and says, "I'll have a turkey sandwich on white bread."

Daniel begins again. "As I started to say, I want to thank you all for coming. You are the people who mean the most to me, and I wanted you all to meet Rita."

Remembering the name Rita from so long ago, Pat practically spits out his water when he blurts out, "Rita? Rita from a long time ago? That Rita?"

Rita smiles. "I guess I'm that Rita."

Rose jumps in. "How long ago? We know Daniel longer than anybody. How come we never heard of Rita?"

Daniel says, "Rita and I knew each other in Bukachivtski before we came to America. And now we found each other. And we're going to stay together this time." Daniel and Rita kiss.

Rose breaks them apart by pointing to the room in the back, saying, "Before Daniel became a big doctor, he used to live back there."

Rita says, "Really?"

"Hyman and Rose took me in. They are like my American parents."

Daniel gets up and kisses both Rose and Hyman.

Hyman says to Rita, "You've got a good one."

Then Daniel addresses Pat, Laurie, and Norma. "And when I went to college, I didn't know anybody there. The school put me in a room with Pat and Hoby. And without them, I don't know what I would have done."

Norma likes being included. Pat speaks up. "And Daniel would talk to us about Rita—especially when he got drunk." He then turns to Rita: "But he didn't say too much."

Daniel's shrug corroborates what Pat said. "But only when I was drunk."

Rose sums up the feelings at the table with Jewish sentimentality. "Rita and Daniel, you should live and be well."

*

Like a quiet evening at home for any comfortable couple, Daniel and Rita are in the living room of his home. She is sitting on a couch with Daniel lying down. He has her head in his lap when he stands abruptly and starts into the other room. Rita is surprised by the suddenness.

Rita asks, "What are you doing?"

From the other room, he calls out, "You'll see!"

Rita can hardly wait to see. He returns with a stack of letters, which he has retrieved from a special place in his home office. He definitely has piqued her curiosity.

He says, "These are letters I wrote you from the war."

"You kept them?"

He sits down next to her and plops the letters on the table in front of them. He explains, "I couldn't have sent them, could I?"

She picks one of them up and gently fingers it. She says, "I didn't write letters, but I wrote what I felt about you almost every day in my diary, which I kept in a cedar box. It is the same cedar box that has been in our family since her days in the Ukraine."

"Weren't you afraid Mikal would find the box?"

"No. It was hidden in the back of a drawer where he was too much of a gentleman to look."

"What about Nathan?"

"Even if he found the box, it wouldn't matter. The diary is in Russian."

"You'll show the diary to me?"

'Of course."

"When?"

"Soon."

Daniel studies Rita's face when he asks, "When we're married?" This is the first time marriage has actually been mentioned. She smiles at him. She puts down the letter in order to kiss him as an answer to his unorthodox proposal.

But she adds definitively, "Yes. When we're married."

They kiss again. She picks up a letter and begins to read: *"My beloved Rita, I think of you every day. The countryside would be beautiful if it weren't covered in the cloud of the smoke of too many cannons—"*

He takes the letter from her hand and stops her with "We will have lots of time to read to each other."

He stands and points to the home office where he kept the letters. "And that can be a room for Nathan when you move in, and he comes home for visits."

She cries since Daniel knows what's important to her—to them.

CHAPTER TWENTY-FIVE

Now in Rita's apartment, Daniel hovers around Rita as she makes dinner. He tastes something simmering in one of the pots. "This is delicious. What I have been missing."

She kisses him in appreciation of his appreciation of her cooking. "It's gravy. Now, will you set the table?"

"If you'll tell me where everything is."

He goes into the dining room and listens to Rita call out, "The silverware is in the top drawer in the glass cabinet. The napkins are in the next drawer over."

While he is taking out knives, forks, and spoons, the door opens, and Nathan, now a college student, enters. Nathan calls out even before he sees that Daniel is in the house. "Mom, I got an A on my first essay in English literature, and I did very well in—"

He stops midsentence when he notices Daniel.

Rita enters from the kitchen. It's unnecessary for her to say gently, "Nathan, we have company," but she has said it anyway.

Nathan says, "Dr. Stabinski? Is something wrong? Mom, are you okay?"

"No. I'm fine."

If she's fine, why does she need to see a doctor? It's not accusatory, it's just a question when he asks Daniel, "Then what are you doing here?"

A moment of truth. "Nathan, there is something that Daniel and I have to talk to you about."

Hearing her call Dr. Stabinski "Daniel," it's easy for the intuitive, intelligent Nathan to figure it out. When his mother takes Daniel's hand tenderly, it is confirmed.

"You and Dr. Stabinski?"

As softly as she possibly can, Rita tells her son, "I like Daniel very much."

A "What?" from Nathan.

Rita finishes her thought. "In fact, I love him."

Up until that moment, Nathan had never considered his mother a woman who could have those kinds of feelings for anyone other than his poppa. "But Poppa's only been gone a few months."

Daniel doesn't dare intercede in the conversation. For now, this must be between Rita and Nathan.

She says, "I know that, but—"

Nathan isn't prepared to hear this kind of news so bluntly. He reacts defiantly. "This ... this isn't right."

Daniel hears Nathan's tone and feels he has to say something. "Nathan, I love your mother, and we want to get married."

"What? You can't. I won't have it. Mother, how dare you! So soon?"

Daniel tries to calm Nathan. "I can understand how you feel. It has to be a surprise for you."

"No, not a surprise. A shock is what it is."

Daniel takes a moment before he says, "That's why I came here today. I knew you'd be coming home. I came here to ask you if it would be all right with you."

Nathan is not about to be calmed down and answers quickly. "Well, it's not."

Rita has never seen Nathan so adamant about anything. She tries to get him to understand. "Nathan, I loved your poppa with all my heart, but as much as it is hard for us, he's gone. Daniel is a very good man. And I love him too. Your poppa wouldn't want me to be alone. You're at college. You are beginning a life for yourself. I want to do the same. I should be allowed to."

The concept of her mother marrying someone else is so hard to grasp. "I just came home to visit. I didn't expect—"

The sentence hangs in the air. Daniel puts an end to the three-way discussion when he tells them both, "I think I'll go now. I can see that the two of you need to talk."

Nathan says curtly, "Yes. Go."

Rita kisses Daniel. Nathan sees this, and this too seems an abhorrent violation for Nathan.

Rita says to Daniel as he leaves, "I will talk to you later."

There is a sudden wall between Rita and Nathan as they stare silently at each other. Rita finally says softly, "That wasn't very nice of you."

Nathan isn't as gentle when he responds, "What'd you expect?"

"I expected you to be nice to Daniel."

"Seeing Dr. Stabinski here like this ... I am barely able to deal with Poppa dying, and now you turn your back on him."

"I'm not turning my back on your poppa. I'm trying to move ahead. And I am going to marry Daniel."

Nathan braces himself. "Whether I like it or not? Is that what you mean? At least Dr. Stabinski asked if I'd be all right with it. Well, I'm not."

Again, silence between them. She touches his brow. He recoils, then he relents, and then Nathan starts to cry. She brings him to her and hugs him. Rita says, "This doesn't mean you should forget Poppa."

Backing away, Nathan says, "I will never forget my father."

For the moment, she puts aside the irony that Nathan doesn't know who his real father is. She puts her arms around him again and says, "I would hope you would understand."

Nathan says through his tears, "I'll try to understand. But I need you to understand how I feel."

"I do. More than you know."

*

So many friends and family from both sides fill Congregation Rodeph Sholom. Also in attendance are all the temple members since a wedding in the synagogue traditionally is open for everyone in the congregation. There are snide whispers between some of the pettier members who think that Rita has not waited long enough after Mikal's death. Even more gossipy attendees think that Rita is marrying the rich Doctor Daniel for his money. The ones who know them well pay no attention to those kinds of comments. All the people who are important to both Rita and Daniel are in the synagogue. Rita is grateful that all of Mikal's family is there. She is pleased that they are blessing her new marriage by coming to the wedding. In that same way, she is glad that all of the people who worked with Mikal at New World Lights and Lamps accepted the invitations. Rita is sad that her mother didn't live to see this day.

From Daniel's side, many of the hospital staff are there. And people from his college and med school days and a few he got close to in the army have come to the wedding.

Rabbi Horowitz, who had officiated at Nathan's bar mitzvah ceremony and Mikal's funeral, waits for the wedding service to begin. In the foyer, the ushers include Pat and Fred from the army. Ruth is the matron of honor. Rita has asked Josef and Goldie to walk her down the aisle, and she is touched that they accepted. Hyman and Rose will walk Daniel down the aisle. Though the wedding party is ready to begin, there is a delay of some kind.

In a room where Rita waits with the bridesmaids and Ruth, Rita is anxious about something and asks Ruth, "Have you seen Nathan?"

Thinking: *Oh, my God. Isn't Nathan here?*, Ruth leaves the room, checks the foyer, scans the congregation, and returns to Rita. "No. I don't see him."

Rita says firmly, "Ask David."

Ruth finds David sitting next to Aaron in the sanctuary. "Have you seen Nathan?"

David and Nathan have remained close friends all these years. They have always confided in each other. David knows where Nathan is. He tells Rita, "Nathan said he'd be here on time."

Ruth pushes David to answer. "He's not here. Where is he?"

David divulges something that Nathan had asked him not to say: "He went to see Mr. Glass."

That's all she needed to hear. Ruth leaves David and goes to Rita in the bridal room. She tells Rita, "Nathan is at the cemetery."

Rita knows her son. Of course, that's where he'd be. With Ruth trailing after her, Rita leaves the bridal room and finds Daniel. She tells him, "Nathan's at the cemetery. I won't get married without him."

Daniel agrees immediately. "Of course not."

Daniel turns to Ruth, "Would you tell everyone to wait? There will be a wedding, but it may take a few minutes."

Ruth says, "I will."

Then Daniel takes Rita's hand. "Let's go."

Rita says, "You don't have to go."

"Yes, I do."

It would be an odd sight for any late arrivals to see the bride and groom dressed in their wedding finery run away from the wedding while all the guests and the wedding party are inside the sanctuary.

*

Nathan is at Mikal's unmarked grave. According to Jewish custom, there is no headstone for a year. Nathan is standing at Mikal's grave, which is next to the marker for Abraham Rabinowich, Rita's father, and her mother, Esther. Nathan, talking to Mikal's grave, says, "Poppa, I want to do what's right, but I don't know what that is."

Rita and Daniel drive in and, so as not to disturb Nathan, park twenty-five yards away. They carefully walk to him. He stops talking when he sees them. Rita and Daniel reach him, and Rita says quietly, "Nathan ..."

Nathan is not defiant. He explains, "I had to come here."

Rita says, "I know."

Nathan says, "Are you angry with me?"

Rita says, "No. I understand."

Then Daniel adds, "We both came here this morning."

This statement catches Nathan by surprise. "You 'both' were?"

Rita says, "That's right."

Nathan responds by breaking into sobs. They let him cry it out. After a minute, Rita embraces her son. Nathan now knows what's right: going to his mother's wedding to someone who will give her a new life. Nathan looks toward the car, which is enough of a signal to Daniel, who says, "The car is right here, if you're ready."

Nathan says, "I'm ready."

With their arms around each other, the three walk from the grave.

*

In the synagogue, Ruth stands next to the rabbi in front of the huppah and holds forth to keep the attendees of the wedding from growing restless. She is telling the crowd anecdotes of her own life leading up to the time she met Rita. "So that's how David and I met Nathan and Rita. I always watched them swing back and forth on the swings. Personally, I always thought David was just a little cuter, but Rita, she thought that—"

She stops herself when she looks to the rear of the synagogue. Daniel is there waving to let Ruth know they are back and ready to proceed. Ruth is relieved. She finishes up with, "Enough about me. I'm sure you all would much rather see a wedding. That's why we're all here. Am I right?"

Ruth leaves the huppah and the confused wedding guests and joins the wedding party. She approaches Rita. "Thank God you're here. I was running out of things to say."

The temple organist starts to play *Mahler's Symphony #3* to begin the ceremony. Hyman and Rose move to stand on either side of Daniel. She kisses Daniel on the cheek before they walk down the aisle together to the front of the congregation to take their places. Daniel looks beyond the rear of those gathered to where Rita stands behind the bridesmaids. Their eyes lock. They have come so far.

Though the ceremony necessarily requires bridesmaids, Daniel wishes all of that would speed up. The bridesmaids, who are all of her sisters-in-laws, move to take their places. Now, there is a pause. All eyes look to see why there is a delay. Then the best man, Nathan, moves down the aisle to stand next to Daniel. Those who know how close Nathan was to Mikal sob. Daniel embraces Nathan and tells him, "Thank you. I love you."

Now all eyes look to the rear of the synagogue, where Rita walks toward Daniel and her future. It was a walk they believed she would make so many years ago in the Ukraine, and now their marriage dream finally is a reality. Each of her steps brings her one step closer. As soon as she reaches him, Daniel turns to Rita and in Russian whispers, *"I love you."*

Rita whispers back in English, "Like I always told you." And then says in Russian, *"No one could love you as much as I do. I always have, and I always will."*

The rest of the wedding and the ensuing party continue. It's celebratory in every way. The people of their lives drink, dance and congratulate Daniel and Rita. The few that know the happy newlywed's truth keep that to themselves. Nothing overshadows the joy that finally has come to Daniel and Rita. Each time someone else wants to dance with Rita, Daniel hides the fact that now that he is with Rita, he doesn't want to share her.

There are the toasts. Ruth says, "Let me just toast the bride and groom. That's all I'm going to say. You've all heard enough from me."

All laugh and drink up.

Pat says, "I never gave a toast at a Jewish wedding before. Just let me say this: "Daniel, you're the best man I know. And Rita, it took a while, but he was worth the wait, right?" And then he mispronounces "mazel tov."

Obviously, all are waiting to hear what Nathan has to say. He stands and says, "I'm not old enough to drink." Then he pauses to find the right words. Finally, he says, "To my mom: She deserves happiness again." And he says, "To Daniel. I really like you now. And I will do my best to learn to love you."

Daniel and Rita realize how difficult all of this is for Nathan. They both kiss and hug him.

Ruth calls out, "Let's all drink to that."

All do. The wedding is a success, and everyone is sure that the marriage will be as well.

*

The wedding festivities are over. Nathan has gone back to college. And even before Rita has moved all her belongings into Daniel's house, and before she has sold her home, she and Daniel have a week for a honeymoon. Daniel has only so much time away from the hospital, so they go to Atlantic City. They wanted to spend these days in a vacation spot with an ocean. The ocean has meant so much to them. On the first evening there, they go to the boardwalk. Rita has brought her diary. She wants Daniel to know how much she thought of him during their time apart. That's what they both have taken to call their years of separation: "Our time apart."

On a bench in front of the Traymore Hotel and facing the ocean, Rita opens the cedar box and hands him her diary. It is in Russian, and no one had ever read it before. No one was supposed to. In fact, Rita herself never reread anything once she made an entry. He asks, "What page would you have me read?"

"Pick any page. In time, you can read it all."

Daniel asks, "Are you going to keep writing in your diary?"

She smiles. "I won't have to. That diary was mostly about how I felt when we were apart. Now that we are together, I have you. And that's better than a diary."

He kisses her in appreciation. She says, "And since you let me read all your letters …"

He laughs. "I had to. They were written to you."

He thumbs through the diary and picks an arbitrary page. He reads Rita's thoughts written in Russian: *And that is why you need to come back. You are what I think about when I close my eyes at night and when I wake up. If we are never to be together again, I would be happy to know just that you are alive and well. That would not be enough, but it would have to be enough. I love you forever.*

They sit in silence. They watch the waves break on the beach. Every so often, a bigger wave comes in and overtakes the small, receding wave, as if it were triumphant. Rita says, "Do you think our engagement was long enough?"

Daniel says, "It depends on how you look at it. I think thirty-one years was long enough for an engagement."

She laughs. They kiss again. Once more, their attention is drawn to the waves. Rita thinks about their journey, and then her thoughts turn to the secret they are keeping from their son. Daniel knows her so well and can tell by the sudden change in her expression what she is thinking.

He asks, "How are we going to tell Nathan?"

She asks, "You mean tell him that you are his real father?"

"Yes. He has to know."

She thinks about it. Does he? Does Nathan have to know? It's not that the issue hasn't occurred to her. Daniel doesn't know it, but she already has made a decision. She says, "My son has two fathers. They both have always been good and honorable men. Nathan loved Mikal, and he will love you. I do, and he will. One is his father; one is his stepfather. Does it really matter which of you was which? Telling him would only hurt him."

Daniel can only say, "You are so wise."

CHAPTER TWENTY-SIX

Daniel and Rita begin their newly uninterrupted life together. Rita and Daniel's old friends, as well as their new friends, can't believe these two met and married so recently. To them, Daniel and Rita are as comfortable with each other as any couple who had been married for a long time.

Nathan isn't home much. He graduated from New York University and was accepted at Columbia Law School, which made his mother very proud. He occasionally stops by the home where Daniel has provided a room for him. Still, Nathan has difficulty adjusting to his mother with a different husband. "It will take time." That's what Rita and Daniel tell each other.

Then, once after a visit over one weekend, Nathan accidentally calls Daniel "Poppa." All of them freeze. Poppa is what Nathan called Mikal. Daniel is the first to suggest that Nathan finds something to call him. Nathan turns it over to Daniel when he asks, "What would you like me to call you?" Nathan systematically lays out the possibilities: Dad, Daddy, Father, Pops, Pop, Abba, or just Daniel. Nathan provides pros and cons for each of the names. Yes, Nathan will make a good lawyer.

Daniel says, "If it were up to me, I think I'd like you to call me Dad."

Nathan mulls that over. Then he says, "I'll try it … 'Dad.'"

Nathan takes the laundry that Rita has done for him and starts to leave to return to law school. He stops to kiss his mother and then prepares to shake hands with Daniel. Instead, Daniel embraces Nathan warmly. Nathan accepts and appreciates the gesture and says, "See you soon … Dad."

It's a breakthrough. After Nathan leaves, Daniel tells Rita, "I've been waiting his whole life for him to hug me."

*

For the first time, Rita invites Ruth to her new home. Ruth is duly impressed. Rita shows her the room that is now Nathan's room. This inspires the irrepressibly nosy Ruth to ask, "How is it between Nathan and Daniel?"

Ruth is Rita's best friend, but she still has to be cautious as to how much she tells Ruth: "They are getting used to each other."

Ruth says, "That's all you're going to say?"

"That's right."

Ruth now wanders into the kitchen and sees that it is first class with all the latest appliances. Ruth names them: "An O'Keefe and Merritt oven, a Frigidaire refrigerator, and a Whirlpool dishwasher. You have it all."

Rita tells her, "Before I moved in, Daniel barely used the stove he had. He left the kitchen up to me, and now it's like this."

Ruth comments, "You have a wealthy doctor husband and a son who is going to be a lawyer. You know what I call that? The Jewish jackpot."

They both laugh. Rita says, "You're happy, aren't you?"

Ruth answers, "Aaron makes a good living in the garment district, but I'm worried about David."

Concerned for her friend's son, Rita says, "What's the matter with David?"

Ruth explains, "Your Nathan is going to be a lawyer. My David is studying English. He wants to be a writer. God help him."

Rita says, "What's the matter with that? David is smart."

Ruth says, "An attorney is someone people go to. He can put up a shingle, "Nathan Glass: Attorney." But a writer? Where can he put that sign? Who will go to him?"

*

Indeed, David and Nathan have remained close all these years. And they are supportive of each other. Nathan reads everything that David writes, and Nathan makes incisive and encouraging suggestions that David feels improves his writing. In turn, David helps Nathan study for his exams. One evening they are together in David's dormitory room at his college. David tells Nathan, "My mother doesn't want me to be a writer."

Nathan says, "Has she ever read what you write?"

"No. I think she's afraid to. She's afraid she might not like it."

"Mothers worry. That's what she is doing. You shouldn't listen to her. You're talented. Shakespeare's mother probably worried about him too."

Nathan and David have similar taste in the girls they date—in fact, similar taste to the extreme. David and Nathan are dating identical twins, Linda and Darlene Gold.

*

Rita and Daniel are home one evening. They have just finished dinner, and Daniel sees that his belt size has increased one notch. "If you keep feeding me like this, I won't fit into my lab coat."

Rita kids him. "So you want me to stop cooking?"

Daniel kids back. "No. I'll just buy a bigger lab coat." Then Daniel says, "Did Nathan say why he was coming by?"

"He said he wanted us to meet someone."

Daniel knows what "meet someone" means. "Did he ever bring a girl home before?"

"No."

"Do you think it's serious?"

"Yes."

"Aren't you concerned?"

"Not until after we meet her. Then maybe I'll be concerned."

When Nathan shows up with Linda, Linda brings sunflowers. For the moment, Nathan speaks formally when he says, "Mom and Dad, this is Linda Gold. Linda, these are my parents."

Daniel, Rita and Linda all say at the same time, "Nice to meet you."

Rita is touched by the gesture that Linda brought sunflowers. Rita tells her, "Sunflowers. That's the national flower of Ukraine."

Nathan speaks for Linda. "She knows. When I told her that's where you and Dad were from, she looked it up."

Linda says, "That's why it helps to work in a bookstore."

Rita likes her immediately. Daniel does too. Nathan and Linda appear to be a great fit. As Rita goes to put the sunflowers in water, Nathan calls after her, "That's where we met. In the college bookstore."

Linda says, "I couldn't believe he could read that many books."

Nathan confesses, "I didn't need half the books I bought. I just went there to be around her."

Rita says, "Nathan is sly that way."

Linda says, "Sly, but not shy."

To prove it, Nathan kisses Linda right in front of Rita and Daniel.

Linda says, "See what I mean?"

Nathan says, "I wanted you all to meet. After all, you are the three most important people in my life."

Rita and Daniel are taken aback by such a bold statement. And they are further surprised when Linda says, "Nate is the most important person in my life."

Daniel says, "You call him Nate?"

Nathan says, "She calls me a lot of other things, but you don't want to hear what those things are."

He is joking—but not really.

Daniel says, "So, Linda, tell me a little about you."

Linda says, "For one thing, I have an identical twin, Darlene."

Nathan jumps in and says, "Who David is seeing."

Rita says, "Isn't that something. How do you and David tell them apart?"

Linda says, "Nate doesn't have to. I just grab his hand." She does so to demonstrate.

The rest of the evening is just as carefree. It is clear that Linda has captured Nathan's heart, and by the end of the evening she has won over Rita and Daniel as well. The event is cut short when Nathan says, "Sorry, we'd love to stay longer, but we have to go now."

Rita says to Nathan, "Do you have to study?"

Linda says, "No, he doesn't. We have to go to my parents'. I want them to meet Nate."

A look is exchanged between Daniel and Rita. Meeting Linda's parents? Obviously, Nathan and Linda are very serious about each other. It is sealed when Nathan says, "And if that goes as well as this, then we want you all to meet each other."

Nathan kisses both Rita and Daniel. "Bye, Mom. Bye, Dad."

Then Linda kisses them both as well, another surprise for Rita and Daniel. "Bye. So nice to finally get to meet you."

Nathan says, "I was waiting until—" He decides not to finish the sentence.

And they're out the door and gone.

Rita and Daniel laugh.

Daniel says, "Finally get to meet us?"

And Daniel quotes Nathan: "'I was waiting until—I wonder how long they've been seeing each other."

Rita says, "We've lost Nathan."

Daniel says, "What do you think?"

Rita says, "I'm not concerned. I really like her. If this is who he wants, I'm fine with it."

Daniel says, "You like her because she is so much like you."

Rita says, "What? Do you really think that's it?"

"Sunflowers. Do you remember our hill and the sunflowers? While she was trying to impress us, that's what I was remembering the whole time they were here."

"So was I."

Daniel and Rita kiss as they are lost in the memories of their love and the future of their son's newfound love.

*

Years go by. And age creeps up on Daniel and Rita and all the people in their lives. There are more ceremonies, some joyous, such as bar mitzvahs, and some sorrowful, such as funerals.

One night, Daniel and Rita are invited to the deli by Rose and Hyman. When they walk in, they see Hyman who is moving slowly. Jerome has taken over more and more of the responsibility, which allows Hyman to join Daniel, Rita, and Rose at the table. After Daniel kisses them hello, as does Rita, Hyman gets to the point of why he wanted to see Daniel.

Hyman says, "Before I tell you what I want to tell you, do you want something to eat? At least a sandwich?"

Daniel says, "No thanks. Rita made dinner."

Rose pats Rita's hand and says, "Good for you."

Then Hyman says, "Daniel, even though you're my doctor—and a good doctor—I don't think you can keep me alive forever."

Rose nudges her husband. "Get to the point, Hyman."

Hyman says, "Rose and I have been talking. What's important to us? This deli is important. We have built it from the ground up. It's almost as important to us as the two of you are."

Daniel is almost brought to tears. "We know that."

Rose says, "After we lost our Leon—" She starts to cry. Though Leon died so long ago, his memory still brings her to tears. Hyman takes her hand. This gesture helps give her the composure to continue. "We loved Leon, and then you came to us. You were God's gift to us."

Hyman takes over since Rose can't. "And we got to thinking: When we're gone, we want you to own and take over Greenbaum's Delicatessen."

Not what Daniel or Rita expected to hear. Now how to respond? Daniel, the chief resident of a major New York hospital, doesn't see himself owning and running a deli. At the same time, he doesn't want to hurt the feelings of the people who have been like parents to him. Daniel says gently, "This place means so much to you. I'm honored."

Rose says, "That's why we want you to have it. You used to live back there. You've seen it grow to what it is today."

An understanding look passes between Daniel and Rita. And then, with as much tenderness as he can summon, Daniel says, "Hyman and Rose, you are like a mother and father to me, and what you're offering is beyond generous. But if I were to take the deli, I'd want to do what you have done—to be here and be just as dedicated as you have been. But if I did that, I'd let down the people at the hospital. And one of the reasons I became a doctor was to make you both proud."

Rose says, "We are so proud."

Hyman, "Still, we have to make plans. What do you think we should do?"

They sit silently as Jerome comes by the table. "Can I get you something? How about some pickles? We have new ones just in."

Rose says, "Thank you, Jerome. But no."

They all watch Jerome as he goes back to his deli responsibilities. Daniel says, "Jerome has been a good worker for you?"

Hyman says, "The best."

Rita remembers how well Jerome worked at Mikal's store as well. "He's always been a good, loyal worker."

Hyman says, "He does so much here. Greenbaum's Deli means almost as much to him as it does to us."

Rose says to her husband, "Do you hear yourself?"

All eyes turn to Jerome, who is helping a customer. Could Hyman and Rose really be this spontaneous? Nods all around. Now all anticipate what Hyman is about to suggest.

He calls off, "Jerome, can I talk to you for a minute?"

Jerome comes over and stands by the table.

Hyman says, "Sit down."

In disbelief, Jerome says, "With all of you? Here?"

Hyman says, "Yes. Here."

Rose adds, "Sit."

Jerome sits. Rose asks him, "Jerome, how long have you worked here?"

Jerome says, "Eight years. And I've loved every minute of it."

Now they know that they are about to make their loyal worker happy beyond happy. Hyman says, "We want to give you the deli."

Jerome can't believe what he is hearing. "What?"

Rose continues the thought. "After we're gone—and that will be a long time from now, God willing—we want you should have Greenbaum's Deli."

The overwhelmed Jerome says, "I don't know what to say."

Hyman says, "Say yes. Just as long as you promise never to change the name Greenbaum's Delicatessen. Now, go back to the customers. You've got work."

Jerome fairly shouts, "I promise. And yes!"

He yells "Yes!" so loudly that everyone in the deli looks at Jerome, who is embarrassed by his own outburst and says, "I'm sorry." Then he goes back to work and is more joyful than any man has ever been.

Rose tells Daniel and Rita, "But he'll have to give you anything to eat you want whenever you come in. Nathan too. That will be part of the deal."

Hyman and Rose are content they have done the right thing.

*

Lives intertwine. When the hora was played at Rita and Daniel's wedding reception, the Jewish people got into it enthusiastically like they always do, holding hands and kicking in a line as they whirled through the reception hall.

Many people at the wedding were not Jewish, and the wedding and the traditions were new to them. Willum watched the hora. Norma, Hoby's widow, watched as well. Then, the spirit took Willum, who decided to jump in. When he spotted Norma alone on the sidelines, he asked her to join him. "I don't know what they're doing, but would you like to dance?"

Norma smiled at him. "Let's give it a try." So, they did, and when she took his hand, they both felt an electricity.

Rita and Daniel were happy to attend the wedding of Willum and Norma. As they told the happy couple when they responded to the invitation, "Happy to attend. You came to ours, so we'll come to yours." Rita and Daniel were so much a part of the lives of Norma and Willum that when they had a daughter, they named her Daniella.

*

A few years later, after more life-changing events, two very special weddings had to be planned. Actually, it was one wedding as the twin sisters, Linda and Darlene, would be marrying Nathan and David in a double ceremony. It would only be right for the twins to marry at the same time. They've done everything together. The wedding would be a happy one for Daniel and Rita, but it would be both happy and bittersweet for Ruth.

David had become a successful writer of articles for magazines. Out in Hollywood, they were looking for writers for the motion picture business. Right after the wedding, David and Darlene would board the train to California, where they would take up residence. For Ruth, such a big distance from David won't be easy.

But the wedding had to come first. There was a large gathering of people just to plan the event. Daniel and Rita and Aaron and Ruth meet with Max and Doris, the parents of Linda and Darlene. Also, there are the prospective brides and grooms. Of course, they all meet at Greenbaum's Deli, where Jerome is only too happy to put together a table—a very large table. Jerome arranges everything for the meeting. He even pays for

184 | LLOYD J. SCHWARTZ

everything for everyone there. That was part of the deal he made with Hyman and Ruth when he became the owner of Greenbaum's Deli after Hyman and Ruth passed away. Jerome would have done it anyway.

Hyman and Rose died within a week of each other. Not only did Jerome fulfill his promise of keeping the name Greenbaum's Delicatessen, he also named sandwiches after Hyman and Rose.

Jerome says, "It's an honor for me to have you all here since Rita and Daniel have been so important to me. I am only sorry that Hyman and Rose Greenbaum can't be here to see this naches." (*Naches* means a combination of joy and luck and blessing and is just one of the words that Rose made sure the gentile Jerome had to learn when he prepared to take over Greenbaum's.)

Normally, the planning of a wedding is the domain of the bride and the bride's family, but in this case, Max and Doris Gold are only too happy to let Ruth and Rita take over. Mostly because after meeting the determined Ruth, they soon realize that she'd be taking over anyway. As the planning meeting goes along, Rita and Daniel steal looks at Nathan and Linda. They can't help but think of their history and the people that have brought them to this day. Daniel squeezes Rita's hand in that recognition, especially when Ruth says, "And at the reception, the grooms will have a chance to thank everyone."

CHAPTER TWENTY-SEVEN

As they prepare to go to the synagogue for the wedding, Nathan is at home with Rita and Daniel. With love and pride, Rita looks at her two men in their dress suits. She has that look that both Nathan and Daniel know is about to turn into tears of joy. Nathan says, "Mom, don't cry."

Daniel says, "Let her cry. If a woman can't cry when her son is about to get married, when can she cry?"

Breaking into sobs, Rita says, "Your dad is right. If I get all my crying out now, I won't cry at the wedding."

Daniel says, "You'll cry at the wedding too. That's what the mother of the groom is supposed to do. You'll cry. Ruth will cry. It will be duet crying."

Rita says, "You know me too well."

As they are about to leave, Nathan says, "Before we go, I want to talk to you both about something."

Rita and Daniel don't know what it could be. With difficulty, Nathan goes on. "On your own wedding day, when I went to the cemetery to see Poppa ... I had to do that."

Rita says, "We know."

Nathan goes on. "I know that you knew that. But I almost ruined your wedding. And you didn't say anything about it. Not one word. I never told you how much that meant to me."

Daniel looks at Rita and says, "You can cry again."

She does. All three share an embrace.

*

Congregation Rodeph Sholom has never seen a better-planned event than the weddings of Nathan and Linda and David and Darlene. From the plethora of sunflowers decorating the aisles and the huppa to the embossed programs, no detail is forgotten: The matching suits of the grooms, the gorgeous identical bridal gowns for the identical twin brides ... all idyllic. The rows of seats are filled—doubly filled—since everybody has friends, coworkers, and relatives. All the surviving people who had attended Daniel and Rita's wedding are among the guests. It gives everyone a chance to catch up on family news and gossip, which is only cut off by the start of the ceremony.

The first unique part of the ceremony are the choices for the best man and maid of honor. Linda and Darlene have chosen each other. Nathan and David have chosen each other as well.

As is the custom at a Jewish wedding ceremony, the brides and grooms rarely speak. Much of the service is in Hebrew, but the double set of emotions brings to tears everyone who is in attendance.

Nathan was never adopted by Daniel, so when the rabbi says, "Nathan Glass, do you take Linda Gold?," hearing the name Glass brings the memory of Mikal into the wedding as well.

Since this is an unusual wedding, the traditional breaking of the glass is equally untraditional. The rabbi puts down both glasses at the same time, and each groom stomps on his glass one after the other. Bang, bang. Then the Rabbi says, "I now pronounce you man and wife and man and wife. You may now kiss your brides."

Nathan and David kiss Linda and Darlene. Everyone couldn't be happier. To end the ceremony, the rabbi cannot resist a joke. "Grooms, look carefully at your brides and make sure you have married the right twin."

A laugh, followed by a recessional, with the organist playing Beethoven's *Ode to Joy* is fitting since few weddings could be more joyful.

The reception, also impeccably planned by Rita and Ruth, is a party that none of the guests will soon forget. The only awkward moment is the traditional bride and bride's father dance. What to do? Max is the father of both brides. Linda and Darlene make that easy. The brides reach out their arms to their father, who joins them both on the dance floor where the three of them dance together.

All the guests laugh while the odd threesome waltzes/stumbles around the room. That leaves Doris alone. That issue is resolved when Nathan and David look at each other, nod, and both take Doris in their arms, and these three dance as well.

Rita and Ruth smile, and Ruth nudges Rita to tell her, "We couldn't have planned that better ourselves."

The dancing gives way to speeches. Max—not known for his wit—has the best joke in all the remarks. He tells everyone, "I'm not losing a daughter. I'm losing two daughters." Everyone laughs. Then Max adds, "But I'm gaining two sons."

As for Aaron and Ruth … as usual, she does the talking for both of them. Never one to miss an opportunity, she makes an undeniable pitch for the new business that she and Rita are going into: "If you like this reception, Rita and I are opening a party planning business. We have to keep ourselves busy now that our sons are married off." Everyone laughs, with not everyone aware that Ruth and Rita's party planning will soon become a reality.

Rita and Daniel rise to speak together. Rita is about to say something, but she starts crying instead. Daniel says to everyone, "See what I have to live with?"

Holding Rita, Daniel says, "This is one of the happiest moments in my wife's life. Can't you tell?" Rita nods and cries even more loudly as proof. Daniel continues. "As many of you know, Rita and I have shared an interesting and complicated life. But always, the best thing in it was and is Nathan. We wish Nathan and Linda every happiness as they go on their own journey. They should know that we will always be there for them—all of us." In his own way he is including Mikal when he said, "All of us."

All Rita can add is, "He's right," before she keeps sobbing.

Linda and Darlene and Nathan and David rise to speak together. David says, "This is where the best man makes a toast."

Now Nathan jumps in and says, "That's right, I will."

David says, "I will."

A mock face-off. They then speak in unison, "Raise your glasses."

All do.

Then they speak in unison again, "To the best friend and man I know."

People drink when the brides kiss their husbands. They follow suit and also say in unison, 'To the best sister and friend I have.'

All laugh and toast again.

Keeping in the spirit of the festivities, the wedding cake has four figures on it. Dancing and joy continue long into the evening.

*

Even though Nathan had never actually lived with Daniel and Rita, his room was always there.

Now that he is married, and he and Linda have moved into a place of their own, their own home feels different to Daniel and Rita. In an odd way, they are newlyweds since there hadn't been a time when they had a place truly all to themselves.

They go out as couples, with Ruth and Aaron, and with Willum and Norma, and with other doctors and their wives, but most of the time, Daniel and Rita just stay home and enjoy each other, making up for their lost time.

When they talk about their lives apart, Rita occasionally mentions Mikal. And when she does, those moments are unintentionally awkward. After a few times after this happens, Daniel feels he must talk to her about it. "I don't want you to forget Mikal. There is no way you can or should, but please realize that he's not someone I want to hear a lot about. Those years away from you were the most painful of my life. He was a good man. Trust me; I know that. And the situation was not even of his making, but he was the reason that you and I were apart for so long. And his existence was the reason that Nathan doesn't know I am his father."

Rita understands Daniel's perspective and sees how much talking about Mikal hurts Daniel. She tries not to mention Mikal, but sometimes she slips. When this happens, Daniel doesn't need her to apologize. He can see in her eyes that she is sorry, and that's enough for him.

One time when this happened, Rita kissed him. "Thank God fate brought us together."

Daniel says with a laugh, "That's right. Fate and Ruth."

*

While Daniel's days are occupied at the hospital, Rita and Ruth have opened a store for R & R Events. Thank goodness their names both begin with an R, so they don't worry whose name comes first when naming the company. Their store is on the same block where New World Lights and Lamps had been. Each day when Rita walks to work, she passes the space where Mikal had spent so many years. Memories flood back. Occupying that store now is a travel agency that offers ocean trips across the Atlantic to European destinations. Rita shakes her head when she looks in the window where would-be voyagers talk to travel agents about booking space on luxury ocean liners. It was all Rita and Daniel and Mikal could do to leave that part of the world, and now people want to go there on vacations.

R & R Party Planners has a monopoly on all the bar mitzvah receptions for their temple members. And that expands to weddings. Everybody is impressed with those events. Some other events are arranged for non-Jewish customers, so R&R is growing to include baptisms and church weddings. Ruth and Rita don't discriminate; they merely profit.

*

At the hospital, Daniel spends less and less time seeing patients and more time in administration. That bothers him. He remembers a long time ago when Dr. Gregory had told him he was going to be a great doctor. What would Dr. Gregory think now? Still, Daniel knows what he does is important. The hospital has a sterling reputation in large part due to Daniel's organizational skills and his ability to attract the best physicians. He relishes the times when a doctor asks for his help when there is a particularly difficult case.

*

Daniel and Rita love the time at the end of the day when they arrive at home around the same time. She goes to the kitchen, and he stands behind her to look over her shoulder while she prepares dinner. He talks about the hospital and sometimes complains that he doesn't see enough patients. She talks about the latest events that she and Ruth are planning and sometimes complains about Ruth. The one thing they never complain about is each other. They open a bottle of wine and eat and look at each other and marvel that life can be this good.

*

Life gets even better one evening when Nathan and Linda come calling. They are often there for Shebat dinner, but this is a Tuesday. It's clear they have a reason for stopping by.

Nathan says, "We have news."

Linda can't wait to complete the thought, and she beams. "I'm going to have a baby."

Hugs all around. Mazel tovs, too. Then Daniel says, "But we knew."

Nathan says, "How could you know?"

Daniel says, "Remember, I'm a doctor, and I see pregnant women all the time."

Then Rita says, "And I knew too. I'm a mother."

Nathan and Linda are amazed at their perceptions, and then Nathan says, "Then it's not a surprise?"

Rita says, "And we knew another way. Linda, you told Darlene first. And you made her swear to keep it a secret, so she naturally told her mother and swore Doris to keep it a secret, so Doris naturally told me and made me swear to keep it a secret, so naturally I told Daniel."

Everyone laughs. Rita goes to the cupboard and brings out a bottle of wine. She says, "We've been keeping this wine ready for when you would come to tell us the news in person."

Daniel opens the bottle and pours the wine into glasses that have also been ready for the big news. Daniel says, "L'chaim."

All follow him by saying "l'chaim" and then drink the wine.

As they all reflect and talk on top of each other about how their lives will change with the addition of a new person, Rita asks, "Have you thought of any names for the baby?"

Linda says, "In my family, the only relative who I thought to name the baby after was my father's brother Levi, but I only met him twice."

Nathan says, "For me, there is only one choice."

Rita and Daniel both know who that is. Nathan confirms. "We decided to name the baby with the letter "M" for my poppa ... for Mikal."

Rita says, "I think that's beautiful."

Daniel says, "I think that's right. We wouldn't have it any other way."

Linda says, "So the baby will be Molly if she's a girl, and Matthew if he's a boy."

Daniel pours another round and declares, "For Molly or Matthew."

All agree: "For Molly or Matthew."

Nathan says, "Now we have to go tell the rest of the world the good news—unless the rest of the world knows already since they were told by people who can't keep secrets." They laugh since Nathan knows them too well, and then kisses all around until Nathan and Linda leave.

As always, when Rita and Daniel are in bed, they go through the day's happenings. And this day, when Nathan told them that he and Linda will have a child, is one of the most eventful. Rita is proud that Daniel didn't object when the baby would be named in honor of Mikal.

Daniel says, "This is one time I am not jealous of Mikal since babies can only be named after people who have passed away."

Rita says, "Still, you are generous."

Daniel says, "If doing what your own child wants is being generous, then I am generous."

She kisses him. He says, "Sometime—and I hope a long time from now—someone might think enough of me to name a child with my initial."

CHAPTER TWENTY-EIGHT

Things change for Rita and Daniel, mostly for the better. Not only are they enjoying a close relationship with their growing grandson, Matthew, but their work lives are getting more successful for Rita and easier for Daniel.

Ruth is a whirlwind at securing new events for R & R Party Planners to arrange, and Rita is a festival of organization in carrying out the planning. For months, people were still talking about the Epstein wedding they arranged at the base of the Statue of Liberty. It was even written about in *The New York Times.*

At the hospital, Daniel discovered the excellent physician, Ken Pearlman. Just as Daniel had been a disciple of Dr. Gregory, Ken Pearlman becomes a right arm for Daniel. The multitalented Dr. Pearlman soon took over a lot of the administrative responsibilities that Daniel didn't like to do. Ken is personable and has become a valued friend and coworker. Ken's wife, Hazel, is welcomed by Rita and becomes like the younger sister Rita never had.

It's not unusual when Hazel and Ken come over for dinner, but it is surprising when Daniel and Ken come by R & R Party Planning in the middle of the day. Rita knows that Daniel and Ken would not leave the hospital at the same time, so she suspects that whatever they have to tell her must be important.

Daniel says, "Rita, we'd like to talk to you."

The ever-curious Ruth hovers nearby, but Rita can sense that the information that they must impart is for her alone. Rita nods to Ruth, who goes to the recesses of their store.

Rita says to Daniel, "Should I sit down?"

Daniel says quietly, "Yes."

Rita fears are justified when she listens to Daniel tell her about the cancer that has invaded his pancreas. Ken confirms how serious it is. The news hits Rita hard. The life she is sharing with Daniel is wonderful, but now … Daniel hugs his wife tightly as she begins to cry.

Ruth peeks over to see that Rita is in tears. Ruth wants to go to her closest friend, but she realizes this is not the time. There will be a time, but this is not that time.

Rita stands and tries to be brave when she asks Daniel, "How long do we have?"

Both Daniel and Ken note that Rita said, "How long do 'we' have?" and not "How long do 'you' have?" Daniel and Rita are just that inseparable.

Ken tries to be a friend and not a doctor when he says, "Six months," as gently as he can.

Daniel nods that Ken is right.

Rita sits back down as the reality of it is too much to fathom. "Six months?" Daniel is far more worried about how the news affects Rita than he is about the concept of his own dying. All Rita can say to Daniel is, "I love you always."

Daniel says, "I love you." Then he forces a smile to add, "Always has to be enough."

*

Rita and Daniel are going to tell Nathan and Linda their unhappy news after Shebat dinner. Their plan is for Rita to take Matthew aside when Daniel tells Nathan and Linda. The plan gets changed at dinner when Nathan and Linda beam with the announcement that Linda is expecting again. Nathan and Linda are so elated that they don't see the looks between Daniel and Rita. Both Daniel and Rita know that this is not the time to say anything about Daniel's condition.

On Wednesday of next week, Daniel arranges to have lunch with Nathan at Delmonico's which happens to be near the law firm where Nathan has become an associate partner. Daniel greets the maître d' and then sits across from Nathan and looks at him with a combination of love and sadness. By the way Daniel looks at him, Nathan can tell that the lunch is not casual. Nathan asks, "What is it, Dad? Tell me."

Daniel is trying to find the right words. Finally, he begins by saying, "Nathan, you have been the best son."

Nathan hears the words "have been" and anticipates what Daniel wants to tell him. Nathan is his mother's son and begins to cry immediately without hearing any more. Daniel stands in the restaurant and moves to sit on the same side of the table alongside Nathan. Seeing Nathan in such pain causes Daniel to start crying as well.

Daniel says softly, "It's cancer."

Nathan says, "Are you going to be all right?"

"I'm afraid not. I have six months."

"Is that for sure?"

Daniel tells him, "I'm a doctor. It's pretty sure."

Neither of them has an appetite. The waiter knows Daniel from the years he has eaten at this restaurant, and when he comes over to the table, Daniel asks, "Can you bring a check please?"

The waiter says, "But Dr. Stabinski, you didn't have anything to eat."

Daniel says, "I know. I have to get back to the hospital."

The waiter leaves. Daniel and Nathan look at each other. There is such love between them, that neither needs to say anything.

Finally, Nathan says, "You are a great father."

Daniel notes that Nathan has said "are" and not "have been."

*

In the time he has left, Daniel decides to spend as much time with Rita, Nathan, Matthew, and Linda as he can. Rita lets Ruth take over the business temporarily since Rita wants to be with Daniel as much as possible. And in private conversations, Daniel and Rita affirm their decision that Nathan should never know that Daniel is his real father. Let Nathan continue to believe what he has always believed.

*

After seven months, Daniel is close to the end. Ken is in his hospital room and watching over him. Nurses are nearby. It's a sad day for everyone at the hospital where Daniel spent so many years. Ken calls for Rita and Nathan to come quickly.

Rita and Nathan quietly enter a room that is inundated with cards and flowers. Daniel is beloved by his friends and extended family, as well as everyone at the hospital. Nathan says, "Linda wanted to come, but it's eight months and—"

The weakened Daniel nods and says quietly, "I won't be here when the baby arrives."

Nathan says, "Don't say that."

Daniel continues, "Babies are named after a relative who has passed on."

Nathan, "Dad—"

Daniel says, "It would an honor for me."

All Nathan can say is, "All right."

Then Rita comes close and whispers what she said back in the Ukraine, but this time in English. "No one can love you as much as I do. I always have, and I always will." She kisses him—not just a gentle kiss, but one still filled with passion … a kiss for him to remember … to take with him as he leaves her.

He smiles, and the last thing he says is, "Always has to be enough." With that, and his loved ones surrounding him, Daniel closes his eyes and quietly passes away.

*

The baby is named Deborah, and one of the first places baby Deborah goes is to the ceremony at the hospital where they will dedicate the newly named Dr. Daniel Stabinski Wing. Everyone who can attend is there—old friends, relatives, colleagues.

Linda holds Deborah, and Nathan holds hands with Rita, who stands next to Ken, who speaks at a podium in front of the hundreds who have gathered. Ken says, "When Dr. Stabinski learned he had only a short time to live, we at the hospital said we'd like to dedicate this wing to him. He turned us down. Anybody who knew Dr. Daniel Stabinski would know why. He really didn't like anyone to make a fuss over him. Well, Daniel, you can't do anything about it now."

Those gathered can attest to how true that statement is and respond with a knowing laugh. Ken continues, "There never was a more devoted physician, family member, father, grandfather, and husband than Daniel Stabinski. It was my privilege to call him my mentor and an even a greater privilege to call him my friend. I will think of him every time I walk down this hallway. His wife, Rita, would like to say just a word or two before we unveil the plaque."

He indicates the plaque, which currently is covered by a velvet cloth. Rita steps up to the podium and says, "On behalf of the Stabinski family, I want to thank everyone for coming to this ceremony. Dr. Pearlman is right. Daniel never liked to be the center of attention—except at home and in the operating room. And he didn't like speeches about him. He always thought words were temporary. Well, this building is strong and lasting and will be here always. Daniel liked to say, 'Always has to be enough.'"

She looks to Ken, who points to Nathan, who moves to the covered plaque and pulls away the cloth as the assembled applauds. The beautiful plaque reads Dr. Daniel Stabinski Wing.

Rita moves from the podium to stand next to Nathan. She embraces him.

*

One night years later, Rita goes to bed early since she hasn't been feeling well. The next day will be a full day filled with her grandchildren. Now—trying to fall asleep—she looks around the bedroom fondly at the pictures of her family. Her eyes come to rest on the well-traveled photo of Daniel and her taken so long ago in Botosani. Next to the photo is a vase with a sunflower. She always keeps a fresh sunflower there. She looks at it, remembers, and smiles. And that is how Rita passes away.

*

Every year on the anniversary of Rita's death, Nathan and Linda go the cemetery. This year, Matthew is sixteen and Deborah is ten. As always, Nathan bends down and pulls some grass that has grown over the markers for Mikal and Daniel. Between the two is the marker with the name Rita Glass Stabinski. Underneath is "Grita," which Matthew called her, as did Deborah when she could learn to talk.

Linda puts her arms around Nathan since this is always an emotional day for him. They stand there for a few minutes. Deborah reads the marker for Mikal and asks, "Who was Mikal Glass?"

Nathan says, "Honey, he was my father."

She is a little confused, so she asks, "Then who was Daniel Stabinski?"

Nathan says, "He was my father too."

Linda tells her children, "Your daddy was lucky enough to have two fathers."

That satisfies the children, and they walk from the graves.

CHAPTER TWENTY-NINE

(As told by Matthew Alan Glass)

My mother and my sister, Deborah, use the same branch of the bank that our family has been using for years. At twenty, I just got my own account. Deb is only fourteen, so she won't get one for a few years. She probably won't wait until she is twenty since she is more mature than I am. That's what everybody says.

This time we are not going to take money out or put money in. This time, we are all going there together to open Grita's safety deposit box. It's the same safety deposit box that my dad used after her, but he didn't open it very often. Only once or twice that I can remember, and that was to check on a life insurance policy or the mortgage payments to see how many more payments were left on the house.

The new bank manager, Helen Nakasone, knows my mother well. Miss Nakasone even went to Dad's funeral. She didn't have to, but she genuinely liked him. We three barely get in the door of the bank when Miss Nakasone rushes over.

The first thing she says is, "It was a lovely ceremony." The second thing she says is, "I really liked Mr. Glass. He was a nice man."

Mom says, "Thank you. I was happy that so many people were there."

Miss Nakasone says, "That's because he was so well liked. I am so sorry about what happened to him."

I don't want to talk about Dad dying anymore. I have done that for a solid month. It's not that I want to move past that, and it's definitely not that I want to forget my father. I just need to talk about something else—anything else. I say, "We want to open his safety deposit box."

She becomes a banker again and says, "Do you have your key?"

Mom pulls it out of her purse. "Right here."

We follow Miss Nakasone toward the vault where the safety deposit boxes are. After she opens the gate and the huge door, we follow her inside. The place looks like a tomb. Miss Nakasone takes the key from Mom's hand and pairs it with a key of her own and finds the number on the wall of boxes: 6324. She puts both keys in and turns the locks. Then she opens the door and pulls out the large box.

When Dad brought home the envelope before, we never knew exactly where it had been kept. Dad just said, "It's at the bank." I never heard of safety deposit boxes until now. I definitely didn't know what a bank vault looked like inside. It's pretty eerie.

Miss Nakasone places the box on the table. It's there for us to open. She says, "I'll be right outside."

She leaves. We stare at the safety deposit box. Inside is the envelope that has been holding family secrets. We don't open the box right away. Instead, we think about what we are about to do. Once we look in that envelope, whatever is in the contents will be looked at for the first time in a very long time.

Mom sighs before she says, "Let's do what we came here to do."

We open the box. On top of the other papers is the envelope that Grita had put in there. Mom takes it out and says to Deborah and me, "I've had a long life with your father, and he made me promise never to open the envelope until he was gone." Then she adds sadly, "Well, he is."

I take out the envelope and read, "For Nathan. To be opened after Nathan's death."

Deb is anxious. "Let's open it."

Mom looks around at the cold room. She decides, "This is no place to open the envelope. Besides, we've waited this long. Let's take it home. Dad would have wanted us to open it in the home he loved. Not here."

Even though we are desperate to see what's inside, we know that Mom is right. Mom points to a call button on the wall and says, "Ring for the bank manager."

I press the button, and the bank manager appears. She sees that Mom is clutching the envelope to her chest.

Not saying anything about it, Miss Nakasone says, "Then you're done?"

Mom says we are and thanks her. Miss Nakasone takes the box and puts it back in its receptacle. Mom hands her the key, and Miss Nakasone locks #6234 again. I wonder when the next time is that we'll be opening that safety deposit box.

We don't talk on the way home from the bank. We don't have to. Mom, Deb, and I are in our own worlds while we wonder about what's in the envelope. At home, we put the envelope on the dining room table. Around us on the walls are family pictures. Dad is in a lot of them, so in a way, he is watching us take things out of the envelope.

Mom says, "I guess the time has come."

The first thing to come out of the envelope is an old photo. It's of Grampa Daniel and Grita. It's a very old picture. Grita is not even twenty.

Mom says, "This is from when they were in the Ukraine."

I say to Mom, "But Grita always said she only met Grandpa Daniel in this country. That's what she told Dad."

Mom says, "That is very odd."

Then, falling out are letters and a diary. We start to look at them and stop right away. They are not written in English. Mom knows enough of the Russian alphabet to tell us, "They are all written in Russian. Your Grita was from the Ukraine and spoke Russian."

Disappointment all around. We all thought the mystery was going to be solved today, but no such luck. I say, "What do we do now?"

Deb echoes me, "Yeah, what?"

Mom is thinking ahead of us. "We get this all translated. That's what we do."

Deb says, "When it come back and it's in English, can I read it?"

Mom thinks about it a while before she says, "We'll see."

CHAPTER THIRTY

Linda didn't want to go alone to the consulate-general in New York City at 7–9 East 61st Street. Luckily, her twin sister, Darlene, is in town to visit and accompanies her to the imposing building. Carrying the envelope, they go inside together. The decor is austere with a Russian flag and portraits of men with dour expressions. The two sisters face a stern woman at the reception desk, so stern that Linda wants to turn and leave immediately.

Darlene pushes her sister forward and tells her, "You have to do this. This is what we came here for."

Linda knows her sister is right. Linda says to the woman at the desk, "Is there someone here who can read Russian?"

The woman scoffs and says, "Everyone here can read Russian."

Linda says, "Good. Maybe you can help me out. I am hoping to have someone translate some letters and a diary from Russian into English."

The woman has heard these kinds of requests before. "We do not do that here. That is not why Russia has a consulate general in your country."

Darlene steps in. "My sister has a diary from her husband's mother and would like to know what's inside. It's important to her."

The woman softens. "Try the university. Maybe someone there can help you."

Darlene and Linda say together, "Thank you."

The woman doesn't respond further. Linda and Darlene turn and leave—but they could be one step closer. The university is New York University. That would only be fitting since that is where Nathan did his undergraduate studies, and that is where he and Linda met.

*

Still carrying the envelope with the letters and diary, the two sisters enter the campus of NYU and stop the first student they see, a guy carrying a lot of books who is rushing between classes. Darlene asks him, "Do you know where the department is for Russian studies?"

He points. "That building is for languages. Maybe one of them is Russian."

The busy student is off before they can thank him. They go to the building he pointed out. When they enter the lobby, a registry lists the different departments for the different languages. Russian Studies is on the second floor. They head for the stairs immediately and then enter the office, where three students sit on uncomfortable, straight-backed chairs, as they are probably waiting for appointments.

Linda and Darlene approach the round-faced, Russian-looking woman who is at the desk/counter facing the door. As usual, Darlene speaks first. "Is there someone here who can help us?"

The woman looks at the two of them. She doubts it, but maybe they are students. And helping students is her job. Speaking with a Russian accent, she says, "If you want to register for classes, that happens on the first Monday in September."

Darlene speaks again. "We don't want to take classes. We are hoping to find someone who speaks Russian who can do some translation for us. It's important."

"I can put something on the bulletin board."

No. That's not what Linda or Darlene want to hear. However, the interchange catches the ear of one of the students who has been waiting on one of the chairs. She speaks up in a Russian accent, "Maybe I can help."

They turn as Valentina Sokolova comes up to them. With an accent, she says, "I didn't mean to listen in, but I heard that you are looking for someone to translate something from Russian. Is that right?"

They look at Valentina. She looks like she's in her early twenties. Could this young woman be the answer to their prayers? Darlene speaks right up. "That's right. We are. I mean, she is."

"My name is Valentina Sokolova. I came from Russia to study here in America. I'm waiting for my boyfriend. He's an associate professor. But maybe I can help you."

Darlene spills the whole story in a torrent. "My sister was married to Nathan, a man who recently passed away in an accident. His mother kept a diary for many years. She died in her nineties. His stepfather wrote letters all in Russian. There was a message that these things weren't to be read until after Nathan died. These things were all in an envelope. They were all in Russian. Nobody in our family reads Russian. We didn't know what to do to find out what they wrote. We went to the Russian embassy, and they couldn't help us, so we came here. And now you say you can help."

All Linda can add is an emphatic, "Can you?"

Valentina says to Linda, "First, I'm sorry about your husband."

Linda says, "Thank you."

Valentina sees the envelope that Linda is carrying. "Is this the envelope?"

Linda says, "Yes."

Valentina puts out her arms. A look passes between the sisters before Linda presents the envelope to Valentina, as if she were presenting a newborn to its mother. Valentina looks at a letter or two. Smiles of understanding since she can read and appreciate what Daniel had written. Then she reads the first page of the diary. Whatever she reads is touching and soul-baring. Linda and Darlene study Valentina's face and can see that Valentina is moved by what she has read so far. She says to them, "It would be my honor and pleasure to help you."

Linda breaks into tears. Darlene says to Valentina, "You are a godsend."

*

It takes a few months for Valentina to translate the diary and the letters. She and Linda set a date for her to deliver the translated versions. Darlene had already gone back to California, but there is no way she would miss the delivery of the translation. David and Darlene take the first plane they can find to bring them back to the East Coast to be there. Besides everything else, Nathan was David's best friend. He had to be there for Nathan.

Valentina shows up at the home where Linda and Nathan had lived and where Linda and her family still live. She carries the original envelope with the diaries and the letter as well as her translated versions. Linda starts to introduce Valentina to her family, but Valentina stops her. "I know who you all are. I've read about all of you in Rita's diary."

For the first time, they realize that Rita must have been chronicling her entire life, including things about them. Linda shows Valentina the aged photo of Daniel and Rita. Linda says, "This is—"

Valentina cuts her off. "Rita and Daniel. I can tell. I know all about them. I know all about that picture."

Linda asks Valentina, "Before you give us the letters and the diary, did you learn the reason that she didn't want anybody to read these things until after my husband died?"

Valentina says bluntly, "Yes."

With that, she hands the envelope and the translations to Linda, who puts them on the dining room table. Valentina goes on. "I'm going to give you the translations, but I'm not going to be here when you read what Rita wrote in her diary or what Daniel wrote in his letters. I learned so much about who Rita and Daniel and Mikal and Nathan were, and you will see them in a way you haven't before. God bless you all."

Valentina starts to leave, and Linda stops her. "Wait. I want to pay you for your work."

Valentina says, "No. I won't take any money. It was my privilege."

She is out the door before anyone can even try to change her mind or stop her. All eyes turn to the translated diary and the letters on the table. Linda says, "Which should we read first? The letters or the diary?"

Everyone agrees upon the diary. Linda takes a breath and looks at the first page. "My Diary." She reads, "I don't like living in this shtetl. It is gray. Everything about it is gray. The only light here is the young man I love. My papa and mama don't understand how I can love somebody that much, somebody who has nothing and offers nothing. But that is how I feel about Daniel Stabinski. He is my soul, and I will love him forever. Maybe what we did was wrong, making love that way, but it was right for us. I know that, and nothing will change how I feel. And tomorrow, when I marry a man I never met—"

She stops reading as the magnitude of Rita's opening entries in her diary begin to explain why she wanted the story not to be revealed until Nathan passed away. Linda looks at those gathered around her. "Should I go on?"

David says, "My mother would want you to."

Linda returns to reading. "This man, Mikal Gleisserman, a man I don't know, and—"

Linda continues to read the revelations that shaped an entire generation of her family. And now it is clear who Nathan's real father was. There will no longer be a mystery why Rita didn't want Nathan to know the story. But it is a story that Rita felt other people should hear.

The family gathers for many hours to hear the unfolding of the intertwining of the lives of the preceding generations. Some of it is surprising, some shocking, but all of it makes it clear why Rita wrote "For Nathan. To be opened after Nathan's death."

ACKNOWLEDGMENTS

Though this is a fictional story, the content is greatly influenced by the people in my life. The characters are also fictional, but none would exist if it weren't for the people who have been part of my life who have led to this telling.

In sincere gratitude, and in addition to my family, to whom I dedicated *It Might Have Been,* I thank Elaine Leff, Marsha Posner Williams, Lattice Productions, Jerry Houser, Selena Schwartz, Jimmy Hawkins, Joanna Ikeda, Sharon Crigler, Joanie Coyote, Adryan Russ, Mike Blue, and Mike Weinstein.

Printed in the United States
by Baker & Taylor Publisher Services